THE VOICELESS DREAM

CENNET EIHA

The Voiceless Dream
Copyright © 2021 by Fatma Al Arbawi

All rights reserved. Printed in the United States of America. No part of this book may be used or reproduced in any manner whatsoever without the written permission of the author except in the case of brief quotations embodied in critical articles or reviews.

This book is a work of fiction. Names, characters, businesses, organizations, places, events and incidents either are the product of the author's imagination or are used fictitiously. Any resemblance to actual persons, living or dead, events, or locales is entirely coincidental.

For information contact :
(cenneteiha@gmail.com)

Book and Cover design by Fatma Al Arbawi
ISBN: 979-8-731-49316-1

First Edition: April 2021

10 9 8 7 6 5 4 3 2 1

Dedicated to: All of my dearest friends and anyone daring and wise enough to understand the other side

I.	The Village Life
II.	The Patrolling Grounds
III.	A Sad Truth
IV.	The Devils
V.	The Boy
VI.	Broken Thoughts, Broken Souls
VII.	Risks, Risks, Risks
VIII.	Bitter-Sweet
IX.	A Dark Night
X.	Patience
XI.	Danger, Danger
XII.	Better Watch Out
XIII.	Death's Stare
XIV.	Another Day, Another Plan
XV.	Tensions Rise
XVI.	The Last Night
XVII.	Run
XVIII.	The Final Phase
XIX.	Almost There
XX.	Forlorn
XXI.	And Then There Was One
XXII.	And Then There Were None

The Village Life

Being followed by death and having it lurk in every corner of life was something Dalia had always faced. There was always a threat that had to cross her path. There was always some dangerous situation that had a high possibility of emerging.

The one thing her mind had always dreamed of was a normal life. A life where she was free. She heard stories in her village about how pure and sweet every bit of it was. How you

THE VOICELESS DREAM

had the freedom to walk about with no fear. How you never had to worry about hunger or thirst. How you didn't have to run away from an army of people where so many of them wanted you dead.

Dalia wished that one day she could escape her strange life, and save her family from it. But for now, she needed to catch her younger brother before he ran off and hurt himself.

"Catch him, Dalia!" her grandfather called to her.

"Abdul! Come back," she called to him. Her little brother came running to her. He jumped around and screamed. Abdul. He was so different from what most brothers were like. He ate in an abnormal manner. He couldn't speak and only made incomprehensible sounds. He yelled at any occasion he could. Dalia remembered what her grandfather had told her. Ever since he was three, he had been mentally disabled, to a point where he could not fend for himself. Dalia would always be his protector.

Dalia stood up from the cool stone floor of her home. She turned toward her grandfather. "I'm going to take Abul around the village today. He hasn't gone out in ages." It was hard to take Abdul outside of the house much because he would attempt to run off in a senseless direction. Once, he had almost run into a deep hole, on one side of a road. Dalia had caught him at the last second before he had aimlessly propelled himself into it.

"Of course. Take him outside, but don't wander too far. Stay in the middle of the village," he responded slowly. He grabbed his cane that had been laying beside him, stood up,

The Voiceless Dream

and limped out of the small room they were gathered in, his robes moving swiftly around his feet.

Dalia took her brother's hand and began to walk towards the old wooden door of their home. She glanced down at him and smiled a small smile as she shut the door behind them. Her brother had a natural tan tone to his skin, and so did she. His hair was thick and wavy, much like hers, except she always kept hers tied back. They also shared a striking feature; their large dark eyes, the color of brewed Arabian coffee.

Dalia instinctively glanced behind her shoulder. No one and nothing was on the thin cobblestone path, except for her and her brother. She caught a glimpse of their small, lightly colored, stone home before she turned her head back.

The cobblestone path soon turned into a dusty road in front of them that then stretched off about 20 more meters until it split into two pathways, leading left and right. The two roads up ahead disappeared behind many more concrete and brick homes and buildings, just like Dalia's, all lined and pushed close together. The air was warm and the sun shone above them like a bright lantern. Dalia was grateful for her shirt and pants that kept her cool amid the heat. The bright red color of her shirt and her jeans stood out among the lightly colored homes and roads.

They began to approach the intersection of the road. She turned onto the left road, still guiding her brother. Abdul began to hum loudly and shook his head vigorously. Dalia sighed, not even glancing at him, but kept her eyes on the path ahead of them. Only three meters away, the road turned

THE VOICELESS DREAM

again, but this time it only led towards the right. They followed that path and Dalia stopped them abruptly as they came across a small puppet show.

There were four young children there. Dalia guessed they were all around five years old. They all sat on the dirt road, in front of a house, staring at the puppet show. The show's stand was made out of three, medium-thick slabs of wood, and rope, and the puppets were made out of old clothing. There was a girl puppet with a pink dress, and her mother, the taller puppet, she assumed. They both had black eyes and smiles drawn on. Two middle-aged men were controlling the puppets while kneeling on the rough, burning road.

Dalia and Abdul passed by them, but Dalia quickly swiveled her head to look back at the small group crowded there. *If that man had never killed my parents, Abdul and I would be able to have the same moments that those puppets have.*

It had been bad enough that they had died but her grandfather had almost left this world with them. Luckily, he had survived to tell her the news, but he had come home limping, beaten, and with blood all over his robes and bare feet. The sight of him that day was still very vivid and as clear as glass in her mind. It haunted her when she went to bed at night and consumed her during the day. She constantly had nightmares about her brother and grandfather dying at the hands of the oppressor. She had been told from a young age why it had all happened, but it never had made much sense to Dalia.

Dalia shook her head back into focus as her thoughts slipped away and gazed up at the large sky above her. The

THE VOICELESS DREAM

She only went to the patrolling grounds once in a while. She had seen them from every side of the outskirts of her village. It had been testing enough to find time to even visit them.

The patrolling grounds. The roads around the village that the soldiers monitored. Sometimes they even came into the village itself. For Dalia and her people, being who they were had never been easy for them, especially there. They were dangerous places, where if a mistake was made, bad things would occur to you almost instantly, as if unfortunate events only existed there. Dalia called the soldiers ¨ The *Devils* because she had always wished she was just living in a nightmare with these people who wanted to harm her, hoping it wasn't her reality. But it was. And unfortunately for her and her circumstances, since no one would aid her, it always would be.

She had begun to leave for the patrolling grounds ever since she was 14, in hopes she might be able to see her parents' murderer. She knew it was foolish to hope for such a thing, considering the size of the armies and slim chance she had, but she still wanted to attempt the dangerous and possibly perilous act. Dalia knew that if the man who killed her parents discovered that anyone in her family was still alive, that soldier would hunt her, Abdul, and her grandfather down to his last breath, like a dying rabid dog. Her world was very dangerous and twisted indeed.

Dalia didn't need to force her eyes to stay open, even this late at night. Her anxiousness was the one thing supplying her with energy. The road began to lead to three different

The Voiceless Dream

paths. One straight ahead, one to the left, and one leading to the right. As Dalia approached it, she began to keep herself as close to the walls of the houses as she could. She felt the rough concrete brush lightly against her cold and bare arms, and felt a few plants scratch against her ankles lightly.

Dalia had now arrived at the intersection of the roads. She crouched down and looked to either side, then behind her, and finally in front of her. Each road was deserted, with only the sound of the slowly rushing wind seeming to exist in the streets. Dalia followed the road that led straight ahead, heading toward the western side of her village.

The buildings were beginning to grow larger and darker in color. She made sure she kept her footing light, so that the dirt from the road did not cloud around her worn-out shoes and cause her to trip on the many small stones on the path. She feared that this would make her presence visible to anyone she may not see.

Her heart rate had sped up even more. She was nearly at her destination. She had been traveling for several minutes, but as she felt anticipation make its way inside her chest, she crouched even lower and tried to control her rapid breathing. She began to hear faint voices.

Dalia pressed herself against the wall harder, even though she knew the shadows were covering her enough. She had grown so dependent on their existence for so long, that it was as if the shadows were the only thing in this world she could rely on. She kept walking. The voices now became clearer. They were speaking a language she did not understand, but one she had heard many times.

THE VOICELESS DREAM

She was now approaching the markets, near the ends of the village. She felt a sharp feeling of fright grapple her whole body. The soldiers at night always came past the outskirts and a bit into the village. The road split only a few meters ahead, heading left and right, and then straight ahead. And she saw soldiers, armed, walking on it, both to the left and right side. Each had flashlights, and the lights moved in every direction, over every surface. Some of the soldiers ahead of her were walking closer to the intersection, where the road led *towards her*.

She felt extremely uneasy, like she was about to fall off into oblivion. No matter how many times she did this, she would always be scared and anxious for her death. She looked around the corner and saw the food stands against the walls of the buildings, with their barrels, and the road leading from side to side in front of them. The food stands were made of wood and nails, and each with two posts on either side of a slab of wood nailed perpendicular to them, where they all held baskets in them. A few more buildings were ahead, alongside another pathway past the intersection, and then one could finally see the ends of the village.

Dalia hid behind one of the stands as quickly as she could. She knelt on the rough and ice-cold ground, trying not to breathe audibly. Two soldiers crossed in front of where she was hiding, their flashlights guiding them.

She peeked her head from one side of the stand slightly. Dalia had only two ways of identifying him through his physical appearance. She remembered the fateful day her grandfather had come into their home, with blood on his

THE VOICELESS DREAM

torn robes and beaten face, limping every time he took a step. She remembered how he had told her a man had detained and tried to kill him and her parents in a truck. She remembered how her grandfather had broken into tears telling her about the man. How the man had two dark scars: one long scar that trailed from his left palm to the back of his hand and up his arm, another on his right eye. Dalia remembered it all so well, almost as if the memory had been tattooed into her brain.

The man who had killed her parents also had done one other thing to them, and her grandfather. He had slit the same scars he had onto their hands and faces as well. Villagers who had seen others killed had also seen the same slits left on the victims' hands and faces. They all knew it had to be by the same man.

"Ok," she told herself, with the smallest breath. "Now, where is he?" Dalia looked to the other few food stands lined beside her. She tried to clear the anxiety from her head and the sound of her pounding heart from her ears, but she couldn't. It was all too much. She shook her head irritably and moved as quickly and as quietly as she could to the next stand, squeezing behind the barrel in her way, while crouching as low as her knees would allow her to go. She knelt onto the ground again, resting. As she tried to keep herself concealed, she peeked past one of the ends of the stand and saw the camo pants and boots of a soldier in her field of sight.

The boots were pointed away from her. She could not see the ends of them. He was at the stand she was hiding behind,

THE VOICELESS DREAM

talking to another soldier. She had not seen him before she had moved behind the stand. He must have just come.

Luckily for her, his left side was positioned in front of her. As he dropped his hand to his side, Dalia studied it. Not one mark was anywhere to be seen on his pale hand, nor his face. Not all of the soldiers were pale, which was what made searching for her parent's killer at night so hard. But it was the safest way.

The soldier did not seem to have any marks on his face either. She decided to look from the other side of the stand. There, she made sure to crouch lower. She looked up and saw a second man, with his right side positioned toward her. She tried to heighten her crouch and tilt her head up higher. She made sure to squint her dark eyes so that less light would reflect on them.

Dalia examined his face. There was a scar on his eye. Her eyes widened, but she immediately switched them back into slits. The scar on his eye was one below it, not across it. Dalia felt frustrated and tired. She waited a few seconds for the soldiers to pass, and when they did she crouched down again and moved on to the next food stand, slowing to cross behind the barrel barricading her way. She knelt once again.

Dalia knew she would have to be more cautious, because now it was going to be much harder for her to sneak behind these stands. More soldiers were now surrounding her location. Nonetheless, she looked around the edge of the food stand. Soldiers were still walking along the road. She looked in fear at their guns, uniforms of dark camo, and clear face shields. Their bright lights rapidly moved all around them

The Voiceless Dream

like eager eyes. She tried to analyze their hands again. Still no sign of any marks or scars.

Annoyance swirled in her chest and head like a strong wind, but fear still overtook that feeling. Dalia clenched her hands, and then peaked back around the rough wood and suddenly saw something that made her wish she could materialize into nothingness. Her heart dropped and bounced back up, silencing her. A villager had just approached the road. He had come from the outskirts. And as the soldiers' flashlights poured their light onto his figure, she saw that he was very bruised.

Dalia quickly put a hand to her mouth as recognition enveloped her brain. He was one of the men who had been playing the puppet show for the little children the day before! She lowered her hand slowly, as more fright settled into her head and heart, and watched helplessly as the soldiers examined him. Many more of them stopped walking and crowded around him. Plenty of them began pointing their guns at him, as they yelled at the downtrodden man.

"Go!" they yelled. "Get out of here!" The soldiers pointing their guns at him didn't drop them, even as he turned onto the road Dalia had just been on, to enter back into the village. He disappeared behind the wall of the building that the stands were lined in front of.

Then, someone fired a shot. Dalia heard the gunshot echo it's ghastly piercing sound between the walls of the buildings, as it rang in her ears. She heard the man's body fall on the ground with a thump, as he cried out quietly in pain for the final time.

The Voiceless Dream

Dalia put both of her hands to her mouth to stop the screams trying to crawl out of her mouth. She wanted to cry out, but she knew if she did she would be the next to get shot. She watched in horror as the soldiers dragged the man's body back in the middle of the intersection and inspected it. She looked at his body herself, craning her head around the left side of the stand. There was blood splattered across his clothes.

"What if someone slits his hand?" Dalia breathed quietly, in spite of what she had just witnessed. She examined the scene closely, praying for the poor man in her head.

The soldiers knelt by the man, talking to one another. They were still speaking in their own tongue.

Suddenly, a few began kicking the man's lifeless body. Others came up and seemed to tell them to quit it, because they quickly ceased. Then three other soldiers lifted him up, carrying his hanging form, and disappeared behind one of the low buildings ahead.

Dalia felt anger swell in her chest. She wanted to shriek and run away, but she could do nothing. Her throat was choked and filled with her cries, but she forced every feeling she could down. Crying and screaming would only kill her here. She needed to leave before one of the soldiers discovered her. An image flashed in front of her eyes, depicting her own dead body on the intersection. Dalia swallowed a vile feeling down.

She had lingered here long enough. She didn't want to think about what they would do to her and the last thing her grandfather and brother needed was her death. No, Dalia had

The Voiceless Dream

no luck once again searching for her parents' murderer. She just wanted to know who he was. Even if she couldn't protect her family from him, she just had to know. Tonight was not the night she would discover his identity, though.

Dalia turned to her left, so that now she was facing the food stands she had been concealed by previously. She heightened her position a bit and began moving. But as she had been passing the food stand, a soldier walked by at the same time. He had noticed her motion and she had noticed his. He stopped walking, and began looking between the stands.

Dalia felt her stomach drop and her heart creep into her throat. Her eyes widened with fear. A soldier had seen her move, yet he didn't know for sure where she was. She needed to move back into the shadows, before he found her, and did something to her. An image of the dead man briefly entered her head, but she dismissed it quickly.

She moved briskly to the next stand. He began calling a few other soldiers in his native tongue. *He's definitely telling them about what he saw.* Dalia saw them begin looking between the stands. The only things keeping her from being discovered were the barrels and the dark shadows cast by the homes and other buildings behind her. She kept moving with fear in her heart, behind the barrels once again, to the next stand.

"Who's there?" one soldier yelled in Dalia's language. A woman. She was searching between the stands a little ways behind her. "Come out or we will shoot up every stand here!"

The Voiceless Dream

Dalia began moving even faster after hearing this, even though her legs felt as if they were about to break apart from her body. She finally reached the first stand she had been at, near the edge of the road. She waited impatiently for a few moments when she saw other soldiers run to other stands to search for her. Then, she snuck back into the shadows of the buildings. Crouched down once again, she began to run. And at that same moment, the soldiers begin firing. Dalia heard the loud ruckus and horrible sounds of their gunshots. A few food stands fell to the ground as the shooting stopped.

Her heart was racing faster than her. Her eyesight was becoming dizzy from fear. The whole world in her field of view seemed as if it was getting ready to spin uncontrollably. Her breathing increased, and she began panting loudly. She had almost been killed. She had almost ended up like the man from the puppet show, his body now as lifeless as one of his old puppets. She would never be able to get his image out of her head, with his blood smeared across his shirt and his head lolled to one side. Dalia approached the final turn of the road leading back to her home.

She stopped running. Her legs were aching badly and felt as if they had been stabbed. She looked up and glanced at the small area between two houses, shadowed, and out of view, right beside her. She snuck into it, and sunk to the floor, her back against one of the walls. The shadows hid her, the moonlight still illuminating every road, but it was much dimmer than before. Dalia buried her face in her hands and began to cry.

THE VOICELESS DREAM

Only a few tears dripped from her eyes, down her face. She hated releasing her emotions. She couldn't stop thinking of the dead man. What would his family, his children do without him? It was hard to imagine how heartbroken they would be when they found out he was dead. Her heart was heavy with all the pain she wanted to let out, but she just couldn't free that burden from her soul. Anyone could hear her. The dead silence of the night was like no other silence on the planet.

Dalia breathed deeply. She looked up at the dark sky, then at the road beside her only a few feet from the shadows. She picked herself up quietly, stepped onto the edge of the road, and ran down the path until she began to recognize her home. She stopped in front of it, thinking the old, weathered wooden door seemed to be staring back at her in an unwelcoming manner.

"Well," she said quietly to no one in particular. "Tonight I may not have found that murderer, but I saw plenty more people like him. Those soldiers are devils," she breathed with distaste in her mouth.

Dalia grabbed the door by its side in one quick movement, and slowly opened it. It creaked with every inch she opened it, no matter how carefully she tried to push it. Almost as if to say: *Look. Who's. Just. Come. Home.* She snuck back into her house and slipped off her shoes, leaving them beside the door. Creeping into the bedroom, her heart filled with grief and shock, she was relieved to find her brother and grandfather still deep asleep.

The Voiceless Dream

She collapsed almost silently onto her bed, covering herself with her blanket. Then, she heard someone move in their bed. Looking for the source of the sound, Dalia saw her grandfather shivering mildly in his bed. His blanket was not enough to keep him warm. She got up and walked over to him, carrying her blanket, and draped it over his shivering body. Gradually, he stopped. And when he did, she walked back to her bed. She looked down at the thin stack of fabric that she called a bed. She barely remembered the last time she had owned a mattress.

Dalia slipped beneath the soft fabrics and felt the cold floor underneath her, sending shivers up her back. She gazed up at the dark ceiling. Dalia breathed a heavy sigh of exhaustion and confusion. Slowly, sleep took over her, just as the night had taken over the day.

A Sad Truth

The sun had just begun crawling up into the sky. It's rays spilled like liquid gold throughout the village. However, with the sun comes heat. The morning soon became warm, with not much wind that day. Dalia woke up just as sunrise had ended. She looked around. Abdul was still asleep, and so was her grandfather.

She picked herself up off of her bed. Sleep still fluttered around her body, even though her mind was awake. She went to the room where they made and ate their food. Light spilled through the openings beneath and above the small wooden door of their home. The bag that held their food and sat at the edge of the rug that was set in the middle of the room. It was one the size of a bag of rice. She looked inside.

THE VOICELESS DREAM

There were only two tomatoes, wheat seeds, a loaf of bread, and some milk. She would need to go to the market tomorrow. But did her grandfather have the money?

"I'll need to tell him about this when he wakes up," she sighed, and pulled out a small chunk of bread and took out the fragile glass bottle of milk. She felt a slicing pain of hunger all throughout her body as she sat down onto the colorful rug. Her hunger subsided as she ate.

When she had finished she walked back to the bedroom. She heard her brother making small sounds. Dalia walked into the bedroom reluctantly.

Abdul, come over here!" Dalia said impatiently, not unkindly. He got out of his bed and walked over to her. She took his hand, and led him into the place where they ate.

"Sit down," she commanded him kindly. He sat down, plopping on the ground with his knees outward, feet behind him, and his legs outside of his body. Dalia gave him a large chunk of the bread. He snatched it from her hand, and began eating it, but spilled crumbs all over the rug as he ate.

Abdul had always eaten only a few things. That was just the way he was. He would usually refuse any food other than tomatoes or bread. Dalia gave him some milk, but he only took one short sip, and then pushed the bottle away from himself. He then picked himself up and walked, while making sounds, all the way back to his bed.

Dalia took a rag laying at the corner of the room and began cleaning up Abdul's mess. Just then her grandfather walked into the room.

The Voiceless Dream

"Good morning, Dalia," her grandfather greeted in a raggedy voice. "What do we have to eat today?"

"There is only bread and milk to eat for breakfast. And for lunch and dinner we have two tomatoes and some wheat seeds," Dalia answered, trying to conceal her downcast feeling.

"You need to go to the market tomorrow," he said. "I think you should trade the seeds to one of the sellers for a bit of food, and I have a few coins I earned from selling some fabric," he offered.

"Ok," Dalia replied. "Then I'll go tomorrow." Her grandfather nodded, not looking at her, and sat down beside her. Dalia reached over and gave him the last of the bread and the milk. She stood up and was just about to leave, but halted in her tracks when she heard a heart-wrenching scream coming from outside.

"What was that?" Dalia asked quietly, but just as the words had left her lips, she realized she knew exactly what it was.

"I don't know," her grandfather said, "But I will go see. Stay with Abdul, Dalia." And with that he left, walking as quickly as he could with his weak legs, out of the house.

Dalia knew that the scream came from a loved one of the man she saw the night before. She felt an urge to go and see his dead body, maybe to go and console his family, but why, she didn't know. It was almost like the same urge to find her parents' killer. But at the same time, it scared her to think what the man's body looked like now.

Dalia trudged into the bedroom and dropped onto her bed. Her brother was laying on his own bed tiredly. Her head

The Voiceless Dream

was spinning. The man's death, his family's suffering, all of it was caused by those soldiers she had seen last night. She knew their name well, and it had always stuck with her ever since she was young, for it was a name spoken with caution in her home. *The Israel Defence Forces. The IDF.*

The name made her even dizzier and she allowed herself to lay on her bed. She shut her eyes. *Should I have interfered? Could I have saved him somehow?* An image of his dead figure at the intersection flashed briefly in her mind. *All that blood. All those innocent people they hurt. Is it really worth it to those soldiers?* Dalia shut her eyes tighter. *I don't want it to be like this. My identity is being erased by them. I don't need my existence to be threatened any more than it is now.*

Dalia slowly opened her eyes. She stood and walked over to a basket on the other end of the room. Dalia lowered her knees to the floor and sat with her legs beneath her. She opened the lid of the basket and reached inside. When her hand had wrapped around a key, she brought it back out of the basket and replaced the lid. Dalia let out a sigh. She felt so torn. She gazed down at the key in her hand. *Grandfather's key. The key to his home that his family lost.* Dalia held onto the key tightly for a few moments. *The 128 year-old key that will be alone forever.*

She suddenly couldn't hold onto it anymore. In a few swift motions, she lifted the lid of the basket, threw the key in it, and ran back to her bed. She shut her eyes as hard as she could, seeing nothing but darkness behind her eyelids, and feeling extremely grateful no devastating images were leaping in front of her eyes. Her dizzy head began to throb

The Voiceless Dream

and she heard the door of the house creak open and close shut within a few short seconds. But she was too tired and drained to care about who had opened the door and left. She was used to people leaving her anyway.

The Devils

Dalia's grandfather came home when the sun was almost gone, its last rays of light slowly seeping away from the sky and land. By then, Abdul had woken up. Unlike Dalia and her grandfather, he was in a happy mood. He jumped and screamed happily and ran from room to room. Dalia followed him from time to time to make sure he didn't hurt himself.

"So, where were you?" Dalia asked her grandfather wearily.

"Remember those screams that occurred this morning?"

The Voiceles Dream

Dalia noodded. She already knew the reason why they happened.

"Well, it turns out that a man from our village died this morning and I took all of our food and went to console his family. We may not be able to have lunch or dinner today, but they haven't eaten anything for longer than we have," he explained, in a calm, but downcast tone. "Remember to go to the market stands and get us food tomorrow. I'm going to go to sleep. Watch over your brother," he added as an afterthought, glancing away from her.

Dalia nodded her head inattentively and he walked away. Abdul ran into the room, circling around Dalia. She knew it would take him a long while to get to sleep now, because he did not look anywhere near tired at all. And she was right. Abdul didn't start to show signs of fatigue until about midnight and Dalia recognized them immediately. She had almost fallen asleep three times, just waiting for her brother to doze off too.

She took his hand and tucked him into his bed. He stared at the ceiling, with his lips slightly parted, his eyelids heavy. Dalia only had to wait at his bedside for a few moments before he fell asleep. She sighed heavily with relief. Finally he was asleep. Finally, she would get some rest. She walked over to her bed and slid under her blanket. The night was cold, unlike the daytime, but her thoughts kept her heart and mind warm.

She thought about beautiful tall buildings, trees, and plants. She could feel perfect weather all around her, with the

THE VOICELES DREAM

sun hitting her skin with soft heat, and the wind carrying a faint breeze. All around her, she saw people smiling, going about their day, and walking with no fear. There was not one part of their bodies showing any fear or uneasiness. Every part of them was relaxed. And the only noise filling the air were the happy cries of children living together peacefully. She deeply wondered what it was like to feel so serene.

Sleep took over her soul, as she dreamt of normality, but soon after came a nightmare.

Dalia was running. She could hear people running after her. She ran faster. She heard gunshots in the distance. The path she was moving on was cobblestone. It led up a high hill, into a place she could not see, far ahead of her. All around her was pitch black darkness. She could only see the path in front of her.

"Stop!" she heard a man yell. Dalia didn't. Then, she saw something that made her stop in her tracks. It was her grandfather, lying in a pool of light, coming from a source she did not know.

She breathed his name quietly. He was beaten and bruised, with blood beginning to drip onto the floor from his hands. His arms were sprawled out away from his body, his head lolled to one side. He was unresponsive, "No," she winced faintly. "Don't die!"

A gunshot rang in her ears. Oh, what was she thinking? They would capture her, the army would capture her. She began sprinting away again, their voices even closer. Her

The Voiceles Dream

heart was beating so fast, she was worried it would beat right out of her chest. The path seemed like it would never end. And then, it began shifting upward as she ran up the hill. She looked back. She could see them. But why weren't they shooting her now? She kept looking back, not paying attention to the trail and began to veer off of it.

She fell off the path and down into oblivion, as the darkness swallowed her. She could no longer hear her screams and all she felt was the bitter cold smothering her. Her limbs began to disintegrate, and then the rest of her followed, disappearing into the air as if she had never existed.

Dalia woke up with a start. She sat up, feeling sweat settled all over her body. Her hands were clammy. She suddenly felt relief. It had just been a nightmare, but fear and shock were still living in her chest. She looked outside the window. It was early morning, but the sun still hadn't come up. Her body was tired, so she forced herself back into the abyss of sleep once again, hoping no more nightmares would clasp her in their hands.

"Dalia. Dalia. Wake up," someone was saying to her. Dalia opened her eyes slowly, and saw her grandfather standing beside her bed looking down at her.

"You have to go to the market stands today, remember," he said with eerie tranquillity. He walked away before Dalia could even respond.

THE VOICELES DREAM

Dalia picked herself up off of her bed, and stood up. She felt lethargic and dizzy at the same time. She rubbed at her heavy eyes and went to the eating area of their home, where her grandfather was sitting with Abdul. Abdul looked as tired as she felt. Her grandfather had a serious look on his face, but he did not look up at her.

"Now, Dalia, today when you go, I need you to take Abdul with you, because a man wanted to meet him. He informed me he may have some medicines for him. He will be near the milk stand, ok? Also," he breathed, lowering his voice and changing his tone to a deep warning. He looked her in the eyes and said, "The IDF soldiers will be patrolling around the market stands today. Be *very* careful and stay alert. Protect yourself and Abdul well, and do not let him veer anywhere near the soldiers. Try to keep as far away from them as you can, and just try to buy everything we need as quickly as possible. We don't need you getting detained again."

Dalia knew what he was referring to. A year ago she had gotten detained randomly by the IDF soldiers. They had questioned her inside one of their trucks, still outside the village. She had been able to escape an hour later from them by the help of a few neighbors, and miraculously the IDF soldiers had not noticed or even cared afterward. *They must have been finished with me anyway,* Dalia thought.

"Now, the only things I need you to buy is a bottle of milk, three tomatoes, three loaves of bread, and see if you can buy some water too," he finished. "Here are the wheat seeds and coins."

THE VOICELES DREAM

"Ok," Dalia nodded as she took them from him. The seeds were in a small pouch with the coins. Dalia put the pouch in the pocket of her pants. She looked back at her grandfather. "Should we go now?"

"Yes," her grandfather confirmed. "And dress Abdul and yourself in a jacket, for there is cool air about, and I don't want you getting sick."

"Ok. I'll dress Abdul, but I don't think I need one," Dalia responded. "Come here, Abdul." She beckoned him over by waving her hand. Abdul got up and he took her outstretched hand. Dalia walked him to his bed and sat him down. She opened the lid of a small basket that was beside his bed, which held his clothes. She took out a jacket.

"Dress up," she said to him, holding out the jacket. He skipped over to her slowly, dragging his feet. She dressed him up in the jacket and zipped it.

Dalia then took his hand and she said goodbye to her grandfather, which he returned with a small smile and waved goodbye to them. But little did Dalia know what was about to be thrown her way. That she was about to face the biggest threat in her life.

Dalia and Abdul walked down the path. Their grandfather had been correct about the wind. It was chilly that day, and Dalia was still wearing her red shirt and jeans. She shivered and wished she had listened to her grandfather and worn a jacket too.

The Voiceles Dream

They made their way through the winding dirt path, and finally they were beginning to arrive at the market stands. Dalia saw them immediately. They were on the road that ran left to right. There were so many of them. And up ahead, on the road across from them, she saw their trucks and command cars. She felt fear erupt in her heart and stomach. She gripped Abdul's hand harder.

"Don't worry," she said to him quietly. "I'll be here with you." She leaned down and kissed the top of his head lightly.

They began to approach the intersection of the road. The milk stand was on the left side. Ahead of them was another road between the buildings, leading to the outskirts of the village.They both turned, Dalia leading Abdul. The soldiers glanced at them, and some stared. Dalia knew why. She looked at Abdul, and saw he was quietly humming to himself, and he slapped his other hand lightly to his face.

Abdul began humming louder, and Dalia tried to keep close to the stands. Several more of the IDF soldiers were watching them carefully. Dalia glanced away from them. She finally saw the milk stand, up ahead, and also saw a man waiting beside it. Dalia began to walk faster, trying to get away from the soldiers and to the man by the milk stand as fast as she could. But this caused Abdul to break free from her grip. He began jumping, and kicked a few stones up into the air. One of these stones ended up hitting a soldier's chest, to their right.

Dalia froze. Horror rose in her like a tsunami. The expression of the soldier went from surprised to dangerously angry. He called his comrades in a language she did not

THE VOICELES DREAM

understand. She grabbed Abdul's hand, and dragged him away with all her force, trying to reach the intersection of the road so that they could go back the way they had come.

"Hey!" she heard someone call. She glanced behind her back, still trying to make her way among the people. She saw five soldiers running toward her and Abdul. Her whole body was almost paralyzed by fear, and she tried to use every bit of adrenaline her body produced to push her and her brother out of the market area. She pulled Abdul with her as they ran, and they had just approached the intersection when Dalia felt a firm grip on her arm that yanked her back.

"Where do you think you two are going?" a man's voice spoke in her ear behind her. His voice was deep and menacing. She looked over her shoulder, and saw a tall soldier with a mask covering his face, gripping her arm. The mask concealed everything but his eyes, nose, and mouth. *That is very strange*, she thought, and swallowed hard. Right beside him, two more were grasping Abdul by his arms. Abdul screamed trying to resist their grip, but he was too small and weak.

"Let him go!" Dalia screamed at the men. "He's only seven! He didn't do anything!" she yelled even louder. She wanted to cry so badly. Her frustration was rising. The other villagers on the road were trying to leave before they got captured themselves. Others were trying to reason with the soldiers.

"That doesn't matter," replied the man grasping her arm. "Everyone saw what he did."

The Voiceles Dream

Dalia glared at him and attempted to free herself with her other, free arm, but the man caught it, and twisted both her arms behind her back. Dalia felt a shock of pain and glanced beside herself. One of the men holding her brother was putting his gun to his throat, to keep him from yelling. Another came in front of her brother, and blindfolded him.

Dalia's heart sank. Anger and despair were flooding her tortured soul, but she couldn't do anything about it. She began to cry.

"NOOOO!" she shrieked. "Let him go! He's mentally disabled! He didn't hurt you! Let him go!" she exclaimed, with dismay clouding her head and tears spilling down her face rapidly. She looked to her side again, but Abdul was no longer there. Dalia looked farther ahead in the same direction and recognized Abdul's small figure among the soldiers. The men were pushing Abdul, with their guns, into a truck. Abdul was sobbing, screaming, and trying to resist them. He was shaking his head vigorously as he cried.

He tripped just before he attempted to find his way into the truck, and Dalia was forced to watch in dismay as the IDF lifted and shook her helpless little brother, and threw him into the back of a truck. Two of the men hopped into the back with him, and shut the doors. One soldier got into the front of the truck. The last one left, moving away from the military vehicle. Near the vehicles Dalia could make out large military tanks, which now began rolling towards the village. They intimidated her immensely and she began to feel very small.

The Voiceles Dream

The man grasping her arms behind her back pushed her forward until she was back on the path she had wanted to leave through previously. She stumbled, and fell to the ground, utterly confused and torn.

"Don't meddle," the man spat. "Your brother deserved it." He lowered himself to where she sat on the ground. "You're lucky we didn't take you too," he said in a low warning voice. He then turned and ran to the truck, hopping into the front of it. Dalia watched the truck drive away until it had passed out of sight, behind the buildings that were blocking her view.

"No," she breathed. She couldn't yell anymore; her voice was used up from screaming at the soldiers. She wanted to chase the military truck that held her brother but she knew she couldn't. She would most likely never make it or get detained, wasting her efforts. She looked at the intersection and saw some villagers approaching her. Tears spilled down her face, one after another like raindrops from a heavy rain. She angrily pounded her fists on the road beneath her.

"Are you alright?" a woman asked. Dalia looked up and saw several people surrounding her, all with concerned faces. She felt crowded and quickly nodded, standing up and pushing past the people around her. She ignored their arguments of concern trying to help her and ran down the road. She hid herself in a small area between two buildings, slumped against one wall, exhausted. She noticed several small plants growing in the small crevices near her. She gazed at them as she spoke.

The Voiceles Dream

"What will I say to my grandfather? I can't face him and tell him Abdul is gone." She looked away from the plants in shame, as more tears blurred her vision and dampened her dark, long eyelashes. She pulled her knees to her chin and hid her face.

"No," she said to herself. "I have to do something." She raised her head slowly, as an idea crept into her mind. "I can hide until tomorrow morning, then sneak into one of the trucks and go with them." She frowned as another thought came to her head.

"But where did they take Abdul? What if our grandfather comes looking for us? Ugh." She sighed with frustration, as her tears began drying on her face. "Maybe though," she began, pensively. "Someone can help me answer at least one of these questions." Dalia staggered to her feet and left the refuge of the gap between the buildings and walked toward the intersection.

She examined the road leading left to right. Few of the soldiers or villagers were paying her much attention now. They all seemed to have scattered, except for the soldiers still on the road, and the sellers selling more products and food to the few people left. Instinctively, she kept her guard up as she looked away with anxiousness from the soldiers' daunting glares and guns.

Dalia examined the food stands to her left and saw the man she had seen earlier, still by the milk stand. Dalia walked carefully toward the milk stand, trying to be discreet from anyone around her.

The Boy

The truck drove down the endless path smoothly, with the hum of the engine in his ears. But the one thing ringing in his ears louder than the engine, was the boy. He was twisting, trying to let his hands free from the soldiers that were holding him down. His body was flat on the ground of the truck, and the soldiers were kneeling on it. He was still crying, but luckily his screaming had stopped.

"I will beat you if you don't shut up!" yelled one of the soldiers at the boy, trying to keep his grip on the boy's arms, as they tried to move beneath his jacket. The boy kept resisting

The Voiceless Dream

and twisting. The soldier slapped him on the head, hard. The boy began to cry more.

"Why doesn't he talk? Does he not have a tongue?" The same soldier looked back up at him. "Matt, why won't you say anything?" All the soldiers had their stares directed at him now.

Matt sighed heavily. He didn't want to tell them the real reason he himself was silent. He crossed his arms. Instead he said, "I'm just tired. Didn't get enough sleep. And besides, you dimwits, don't you remember what that girl said about him?

"Huh?" all of the soldiers responded simultaneously.

"She said he was mentally disabled, so that must be the reason he can't utter a single word or understand anything you say. You should let go of his arms. He sounds quieter now. The more you restrain him the more he may scream," he added.

"Fine." They responded. And with that, both soldiers holding the boy down moved their knees from his back, and released their grasps on his arms. The boy still had his eyes blindfolded. He picked himself up and sat with his knees to his chin, his hands covering his face. "But that girl looked very familiar. I think she's been detained before," one of the soldiers said.

"Really?" Matt asked quietly. *She has been detained before?* he thought.

"Yes—but if we keep talking I'm pretty sure the boy will start sobbing again. So keep it down," the same soldier replied.

The Voiceless Dream

That is true. He's finally quiet, Matt thought. *Thank God. But, why does he seem so—* But his thoughts were interrupted as the boy began shrieking and crying once again.

"Hold him down!" Matt yelled at the other soldiers. "And you," he scolded the driver who had turned to see what the commotion was about. "Keep your eyes on the road."

He looked behind his seat and saw both soldiers kneeling on the boy again. He was trying to scream. One of the men began beating him to silence his cries. The boy soon faded into unconsciousness.

At last the truck had arrived at the detention center. Here the interrogation would happen. The facility was surrounded with a large, tall wall with barbed wire at the top. It curled around the whole area. The name of the facility was painted in blue in their language on a high spot on the wall, in front of the enormous doors. The truck was examined and then allowed to enter the facility, and soon the two IDF soldiers in the back of the truck had hopped out, strapped their guns back on, and dragged the unconscious boy out of the truck. They entered the facility.

Matt stepped out of the vehicle. He strapped his rifle on to his uniform and followed his comrades. As soon as he stepped into the building cool air enveloped him, but so did its grim atmosphere. Doors lined the dreary hallways. He saw the soldiers carrying the boy up ahead. He increased the pace of his walk and caught up to them.

"So which room are we taking him to?" he asked.

The Voiceless Dream

"I've already informed an interrogator. We turn left, and he's the last door at the end of that hallway. Of course, only *I* was smart enough to do that," bragged the soldier on the left. The soldier on the right started laughing.

"Cut it out, Ran. And quit laughing, Noam," Matt growled at them. They ignored him for a short while.

They approached the end of the hallway, and turned left, increasing their pace. The boy's head moved from side to side.

"Could you hold his head steadier? I feel like it's gonna fall off," Matt complained, trying to look anywhere but the boy.

"Oh, come on," Ran said to him, teasing. "You *kill* people like him and his *head* bothers you?" He started to hold back a laugh.

"Shut up," Matt snarled quietly. Ran must not have heard him because he broke into a large laughing fit for a few moments longer..

They now neared the last door of the hallway. Matt held the door open for his comrades, and shut it behind him as he entered the room himself. Most of the room was dim, with only a bright light hanging overhead, and a table with a chair in the middle of the room. The room was made of concrete, from the ground to the ceiling. And from the shadowed corners of the eerie room, stepped out a man of a thin build with a bald head.

"Hello," he said, nodding his greeting to the soldiers. "Who have you brought with you? Who is the boy?"

The Voiceless Dream

Matt answered him. "Hello. In answering your questions referring to the boy, we do not know the boy's name. He cannot speak, because he is mentally disabled. However, he did commit an offense to one of my comrades."

"That's me," Ran broke in.

"What was the offense that the boy committed?" the interrogator asked.

"He kicked a stone at Ran here," Matt said, while gesturing towards Ran.

"How old is he?" the bald man asked.

"He is seven years old," responded Matt, remembering what the girl had screamed at them.

"So, how am I to interrogate him if he can't speak?" the man asked them.

"Ask him anyway. So far he hasn't uttered a word to us, but he may say something to you."

"But you did say he was mentally disabled," the interrogator persisted. "That may be the reason he doesn't speak."

"Just question him, and then we'll see who's right," Noam snapped impatiently.

"Fine," the interrogator sighed. "Put the boy on the chair."

Ran and Noam set the boy on the chair. His head tilted toward the ground, a sign that he was still unconscious.

"Go get me a bucket of cold water. I need him awake," the interrogator commanded the soldiers. Ran left the room, and returned a few minutes later with a small metal pail filled halfway with cold water. He gave the water to the interrogator

The Voiceless Dream

and took off the boy's blindfold. The interrogator threw the water at the boy.

The boy woke up with a shake taking over his body and gasped. He lifted his head up and looked at the men in front of him with large brown eyes, shining with the fear and bafflement he felt. He began yelling and panicking, and then stood up, trying to run away from the men.

"Get him!" yelled the questioner. All three men ran to grab the boy. They caught him, just as he reached the far corner of the room. Pulling him by his shirt, they led him back into the chair. Ran restrained the boy's arms behind the chair.

"You can see he's guilty. He tried to run," Ran said with a strained voice, trying to keep the boy in place.

"I'll take care of who's guilty and who isn't," the interrogator rounded on him. He bent over the table and laid his hands flat, firmly on it. "Look at me boy," he commanded the small boy. The boy looked up at him, slowly but frantically, trying to make eye contact.

"Good," the interrogator said. "Now tell me, why did you kick that stone?"

He began to make incomprehensible sounds.

The questioner fixed the boy with a hard stare. "Don't pretend you don't understand. Why did you disrespect a soldier?"

The boy screamed loudly, his stress and confusion clearly evident. He continued to scream, trying to free himself from the grasp restraining his arms and hands. He began kicking fiercely, and slid out of the seat, still shrieking.

The Voiceless Dream

"Why you—" Ran began, but was soon pulled down with the boy, hitting the chair with his leg. His grasp on the boy was broken, and now the boy, under the table, began slapping his arms and hands on the ground.

"Get him out of there!" the interrogator bellowed. Matt reached under the table and dragged the child out by his arms. He lifted him up and twisted his arms behind his back. The boy began crying loudly, tears sliding down his face.

"Make him sign the documents. He just hurt my leg as well," Ran winced. "Noam, go get them!" Noam turned and left the room, with an irritated air about him.

"What will we do with him?" the interrogator asked.

"We'll force him to sign the documents, and then we'll throw him in one of the cells with the other men in there," Matt said.

"How long do you plan to keep him in that cell?" the interrogator asked him, as he fixed him with a cold stare.

"A few months should be enough. If he was older, I would have said a year, maybe two. He's lucky he's still young," Matt replied. Just then the door opened.

"Here are the documents," Noam sighed, as he walked into the room, shuffling through them, with a pen in one hand. "The only thing stated in his language is a few paragraphs at the top saying if a trial were to occur, he could have a lawyer. The rest of the pages are in ours."

"Perfect," Ran commented.

"As if he can even afford a lawyer, much less find one. We took him from a village," Matt said in a mocking tone, as Noam stopped in front of him. "And even if a trial were to occur, we all know he would lose the case anyway," he added. He then lowered the boy onto the chair, and gestured for Ran to position behind him.

"Oh, why do I have to guard him again?" Ran whined.

"Because you were crap at it last time, so you can now redeem yourself," Matt replied, with a trace of ridicule in his voice.

Matt took the documents from Noam's hand. He scanned them, looking for the page with the signature line. When he finally found it he took it out, and set it down on the table. Noam handed him the pen.

"Do you think he can write?" Ran asked him.

"Probably not, and if he can't we will forge a signature ourselves," Noam replied.

Matt looked up at the interrogator. The interrogator glanced at him briefly and then took the document from the table, and set it in front of the boy. The child looked down at it tiredly, then back up at the interrogator. The interrogator set the pen beside the paper.

"Sign it," he ordered the boy. The boy gazed at him with a confused expression. His cheeks still displayed the wet trails where his tears had been. He began making sounds, rapidly saying them, almost as if he thought by uttering them, the men would let him go. The interrogator looked back up at the soldiers.

"Sign it for him," he commanded the soldiers. "He's obviously illiterate too. My work is done here." With that final statement, he left the room briskly, slamming the door

The Voiceless Dream

behind him. The boy flinched from the loud sound, turning his head away.

Matt stared at the boy. The boy didn't even try to meet his gaze. He kept making the same sounds, looking only down at his own shoes. Matt took the document and pen and set them to face himself. Then he signed it.

"Who's name did you use? We don't even know his name," Ran remarked skeptically.

"I made up one for him, at least until we find his real name. Then, we can replace the documents and re-sign it with his name," Matt explained. "Now take him to the cells."

Ran forced the boy out of his chair with a push, and lent one of his arms to Noam. The boy tried tugging his arms from them, but failed. He then tried dragging them with him onto the floor so that they could not take him. Ran kicked the boy's legs and body.

"Get up!" Noam commanded him. The boy stopped resisting, his gray and black jacket now crooked on him, and Ran and Noam dragged him up by his arms. *At least he understands that command,* Noam thought.

Both of them led the boy out. Matt followed. They turned many corners, and then went down in an elevator. They stepped out of it and turned left. Behind them, farther down the hallway, were doors containing equipment and files. But as they walked farther away from the elevator, the lights became dim, and soon rows of cell doors, with bars as windows, lined the hallway on the right side. And with them, were two soldiers on guard standing straight and tall on either side of each cell door.

The Voiceless Dream

"Which one should we put him in?" Ran asked, as Matt began to slow his pace.

Matt looked to a cell door near him, and then looked behind him at his comrades. "This one," he said, as he halted in front of the cell and ushered toward it.

Noam let go of the boy and took out a set of keys from the back pocket of his uniform. The soldiers guarding the door moved out of his way as he approached the door. He searched through them quickly until he found a worn out golden one, and clicked it into the keyhole. Ran dragged the now crying boy inside, and then practically pushed him to the ground of the cell. Noam caught a few surprised expressions from the men inside the cell, from the small, barred window of the door, as they stared at the boy in bewilderment. Then he shut the door, and pulled the small door of the cell door's window shut.

The guards that had been standing in front of the door began stepping back into position, but Matt stopped them. "Ran and I will handle this," he told them. "You can go get ready for the next round at the patrolling grounds." The two men stared at him in a brief moment of surprise and hesitation, then nodded and left quickly.

"Why will you guys stay here and guard the door?" Noam asked them. "That's unlike you."

"Yeah," Ran agreed. "Why are we guarding the door?" He crossed his arms.

Matt looked at Ran and Noam with a serious, and faraway expression. He was trying to formulate a lie as quickly as possible. "I just think . . . we should try to guard the cells more often, because more and more of those stupid detainees keep arriving. Besides, we won't get into too much trouble," he fabricated in a low voice.

Noam eyed him wearily, clearly unconvinced of his claim. "Fine," he said at last. "If you insist. I'll go get ready for the patrol tomorrow." He sighed, then punched both of them, on their heads. "I'll catch you later." And with that he ran back down the hall, before Matt could lash out at him.

"I'll get him for that," Matt growled in a low voice. He and Ran then took their positions in front of the door. Both could hear the boy crying from inside.

A Risky Plan

Waiting felt torturous. Dalia felt so shocked and smothered. Her brother was gone, and she hated to imagine the horrid things he could have been feeling or experiencing at the moment. She didn't want to think that he would feel as if everyone had abandoned him, and she knew she could never forgive herself if he died and left this world in pain. Abdul may not have been the most normal brother she could have received, but he was still her brother.

At times he had made her laugh and smile when they played in the streets outside their home, forgetting about the hateful world they lived in just for a short time. Dalia hated herself for not being able to protect him, but she also knew that everything that had happened had been out of her control; everything had been forcefully taken from her.

THE VOICELESS DREAM

Dalia looked at the sky above her, then ahead of her. The sun was gone. Dark clouds loomed above the village. She stared at the few coins she had left in the small pouch. The man by the milk stand had been easy to convince. He had agreed to her plan. Dalia threw her head back against the wall of the home she was leaning on. She thought back to her deal with the man. She remembered how she had come up to him, begging him for help. How she needed him to go and tell her grandfather that she and her brother were in his refuge, because they had been invited to his home for a meal and would need to stay the night because of the storm.

The man had eventually agreed, even if it was a lie. He said he would notify her grandfather himself, even if it meant running in the rain. He had also attempted to give her one of the small bottles of medication meant for her brother, but she had refused because she knew she had nowhere to keep it or put it. To thank the man for the deed he was doing her, she had given him two of her coins and the seeds, leaving only three coins in her pouch.

And now she was here, between the walls of two houses, outside, with an old blanket she had found beside one of the homes as her only shelter from the cold and now, rain. The rain wasn't heavy, but it wasn't light either. However, the smell of the rain and wet stones around her felt so calming. She needed to stay here, so that she was close to the market area, where then the IDF would come to patrol at night. But she didn't know just yet how to follow them.

The Voiceless Dream

"Maybe I can disguise myself," she thought aloud. "Oh, but with what?" She dismissed the idea and thought again. *The IDF patrol every direction. They sometimes even checked every path in the village. How can I—* And that was when an idea hit her like a train.

From the years she had seen the IDF patrolling or moving around her village, she had never seen one of the soldiers walk, or examine between any two buildings. *Probably because their uniforms, and filled bellies keep them from fitting in there,* Dalia thought bitterly, jealousy winding all over her as she thought of how much more food they received. Maybe, she could sneak between the homes, until she reached the outskirts, where she could walk around them and jump into one of their trucks.

"But which truck?" Dalia whispered in frustration. There were different types. Some trucks took her people away. Dalia grimaced as the memory of Abdul being pushed into one crept back into her mind. She took a deep breath and kept thinking. There were many cars that carried the soldiers. *Definitely not those ones*, Dalia thought with horror, and shuddered. Then there were the trucks that carried equipment. *Maybe they could work for me,* she thought.

"Yes," she whispered aloud. "Maybe I could jump into one of those trucks and stay hidden throughout the whole ride. But," she paused, thinking about how she would hide if the men began taking out the equipment. And mercifully, another idea popped into her mind, as bright as a hopeful candle in the darkness. "I will find the largest equipment case, and then hide in it. They will never know I was in their truck.

The Voiceless Dream

I just need to do it fast." Dalia breathed heavily, relieved she had finished her plan. She felt such a tearing, and shameful feeling in her heart. It extremely diminished her self esteem. She lowered her head.

"How could I let you get detained, Abdul?," she whispered sadly, as tears formed in her eyes. "How could I have let them take you?" Dalia wiped the tears from her eyes, before they could trail down her cheeks. *I can't cry now,* she thought to herself. *I have to get him back. I have to save him and get him home. Crying won't do anything.* She kept these thoughts in her mind, even when the rain halted and night began to crawl across the sky. There was no moonlight tonight. The storm clouds still loomed above the village, and a cold breeze was making its way throughout the roads of the village. Despite her position, Dalia still felt the cold breeze. She pulled the old blanket tighter around her.

Dalia was left with only her frustrating thoughts as her company for a few short hours longer. When suddenly, she heard vehicles from far away, and the low sound of the military tanks. Dalia's head shot up, and she made every part of herself alert. This was it. They were coming. This was her chance to go and save her brother! Dalia stood up, throwing the blanket onto the ground absently.

She pressed her back against the wall, turned her face toward the road beside her, and listened. The trucks were coming closer. She could hear their engines. She needed to sneak out from where she was, and move towards another area, closer to the outskirts of the village. But it was dark. She

The Voiceless Dream

had no light. She would need to feel her way around, and use what map she had in her head of her village.

Dalia knew the village outskirts were not far from where she was, for she was near the market area. Therefore, if she just crossed the intersection of the road, and turned left, she should be able to make it past the market area and to the ends of the . Dalia breathed in and braced herself. She moved her back from the wall, and placed her hand on its rough surface. She began walking, and then the rough surface of the wall was no longer beneath her fingertips. She was on the road now. She turned herself so that she was facing the intersection of the road. She strained her eyes and was able to just make out its outline. She ran down the intersection, her heart beating with fear.

Dalia kept her hands slightly outstretched, so that she did not run into anything. Soon, she felt another wall underneath her fingers. She stopped and tried to make out any object in front of her. She could only see the road in front of her, turning left and right. Dalia walked cautiously, her hand outstretched until she felt her hand touch the wall in front of her.

Just then, Dalia heard yelling. *Oh, no!* she thought. *They're here!* Dalia turned herself and ran down the road heading left. She saw a dark object up ahead on the road. But, as she came closer to it, she realized it was not an object. It was a stain. Her heart skipped a beat, and she felt her legs tremble. This was a large stain of blood. The blood from the man she had seen that got killed by those soldiers the last time she had come to the patrolling grounds.

The Voiceless Dream

Dalia swallowed her fear and horror down her throat. She walked around the blood in the dust and on the stone, continuing down the road. She kept on feeling her way around and made a few more turns, until finally she saw in the distance the trucks and large military tanks approaching her village. Just the sight of them caused an odious feeling to flare in her heart and stomach.

She was now in the outskirts of the village, with only rock, dirt, sand, and groups of some greenery huddled together farther away. The lights of the men from the trucks were pointing and moving slowly in every direction. Dalia ran forward and hid behind a bush. *I can't let myself get into the field of their lights.* She watched as some trucks entered the village, while others stayed on the outskirts.

"Hmm," she said softly. "Almost all of the soldiers have their weapons with them. So, if I'm correct, the equipment trucks are the ones that stay in the outskirts."

She watched as men hopped out of the vehicles. Only a few stayed behind in the outskirts of the village, but all of them were near the buildings, away from their trucks. Dalia looked ahead. In front of her, were only three bushes to hide behind, and they were closer to her than the trucks. She decided she would have to try and run for one of the trucks. Dalia waited until the men that were still in the outskirts *finally* entered the village. She exhaled with impatient relief. Then she bolted from the bush.

She ran towards the vehicle closest to her. Her legs ached, but she leaned forward, pushing herself farther, and forcing herself to run faster. Dalia soon approached the vehicle. She

The Voiceless Dream

stopped quickly beside it before she could topple over. She put her hands on the sides of the truck, and made her way to the back of it. She felt around, trailing her hands up, feeling what seemed to be metal objects, and others with rough fabric and zippers. The cases. Dalia sighed with triumph.

She hastily put her hands on a protruding edge of the truck and hoisted herself up. Dalia squinted her eyes, and was eventually able to make out the shapes of the cases. She rummaged through them, all the way to the bottom of the stacks, and finally found one large enough for her to fit into.

Dalia pulled it up and again moved her hands across the case, hoping to find a way to open it. She frantically searched, and finally felt a latch under her hand. She twisted, and turned it, until the case popped open. Inside the case was what looked like a very large gun. She carefully took it out of its case and set it in an opening near her at the bottom of the truck. She then began stacking back the cases she had moved, on top of the weapon. When she finished, she laid her case down and tried to fit into it. It fit her fine, but she had to keep her legs tucked close to her body. She moved out of it. Then, a realization struck her.

Oh no! How will I get out of the case if I need to lock it? I can't just let the case stay unlocked! I'd easily be discovered! she thought, panicked. Dalia examined the latch. She squinted her eyes, trying to look at it. She tested it by locking and unlocking it. It locked when the hook of the latch was drawn down into a hole in the case, where it was then secured. *If I tied something to the hook, I could pull it upward, and it would open for me,* she realized. She knew there were no strings, but she did have two hair ties and a hair clip in her hair.

She quickly pulled one tie off and broke it so that it became a stretchy line instead of a circular band. She tied it quickly onto the hook, with three knots. Finally, she tested it. She knew that if this didn't work, then she would be stuck in a tight case, with almost no air, possibly resulting in her death. She hesitated, rethinking what she was about to do. Eventually she gave in, took a deep breath, held the band tightly, and squeezed herself into the case, then shut it closed.

When she pulled the band, nothing happened. She began to panic. She tugged at it harder, and then the case popped open.

"Thank God!" Dalia whispered as momentary ease flooded through her. And then a light materialized on the side of the truck. She saw five more, trailing the ground. The soldiers were coming. She frantically pushed herself back in the case and shut it closed. She could hear them now, surrounding the truck.

Do they know I'm here? Did they see me? Dalia thought as she clenched her hands tightly. She felt a push. They had moved aside her case, and now she could hear them rummaging and searching for another. The air in the case was becoming alarmingly thinner in such a short time, and she tried to breathe smaller breaths.

"The soldiers don't need any more equipment tonight. Here are their cases. They'll put them back later during the morning patrol," she heard a man say. And then she felt the cases being thrown beside hers into the back of the truck.

The Voiceless Dream

The man continued talking. "By the way, the General told me to tell you that you need to go to the next few villages down the main road. There are soldiers there that need assistance. You had better hurry."

"Understood," another soldier answered. And with that final statement, she soon felt the vehicle begin to move, and the engine shudder and vibrate beneath her.

Dalia waited for a few minutes for the truck to be far from the outskirts. Finally, she pulled the band and she let the case pop open. She breathed in deeply and looked around her. The men controlling the vehicle could not see her at all, for the back window was blocked by equipment. All around her was sandy terrain with a few trees and vegetation here and there, and the sky was still dark. At least she could see more of what was around her. It was probably early morning by now.

Dalia hopped out of the case and sat on top of the heap. *I'm coming to save you.* She began to feel her heart and mind sag with the weight of the piercing feelings and thoughts. *I will make sure that one day we will both be happy, and if not in this life then hopefully in the next.*

Broken Thoughts, Broken Souls

The truck's engine was audible in Dalia's ears, as she remained sitting atop the heap of cases. The sun was just beginning to peek from the horizon, signaling that morning was here. Clouds drifted lazily in the sky, making Dalia feel tired and lazy herself. She was so exhausted and weary from executing her dangerous plan the night before, but she still tried to force herself to stay awake and alert.

The whole ride she had been trying to think about how she would find Abdul. But she couldn't reason anything. Her mind was clouded and tired. She knew that she would need to figure out which cell or room they could be holding him in, but she didn't know how to find him. *I hope this truck ride ends soon. I am getting tired of it.*

The Voiceless Dream

The sandy terrain was still around her but more greenery was beginning to appear. She began to see hills of bushes, olive trees, and some large crop fields in the distance near the horizon. Only a few minutes passed as these thoughts whirled in her mind, until Dalia began to hear other people. Yet, they did not sound like soldiers. These voices sounded like people of a village. Dalia became alert, and then began to feel homesick.

She looked past the truck and saw that they were approaching a village. She ducked down, in between the cases of equipment so that she would not be noticed. She looked between the cases and saw the houses lined, almost the same as the houses of her village. The truck ventured deeper into the village and soon, Dalia also began to hear the voices of men. They did not radiate the warmth of the village at all. They radiated a menacing aura to her ears.

Just then, she heard a gunshot. Dalia dug herself even deeper between the cases. It seemed that the IDF had invaded this village as well. She peeped between the equipment and saw a man and a small girl, breathing heavily, but covered in blood and dust. They were slumped against a pile of rubble, and cords, and beside them were sledge hammers. They soon moved out of her view and the soldiers' voices grew closer.

"They must have been forced to destroy their home . . . " Her voice faded as the last words slipped out of her mouth.

Dalia was taken out from her daze abruptly when she heard another gunshot. She peeped through the equipment again and saw soldiers in front of her, blocking her view like

The Voiceless Dream

before. Just then, the truck turned and then stopped beside the soldiers. Now her view was clear. She saw that the soldiers were surrounding two small boys that were clutching each other. They were in front of another pile of rubble. Their clothes were torn horribly, and they looked scared and angry.

The men that had been driving the truck hopped out and stood near the soldiers. The boys looked even more scared now.

"Why did you do that! Huh?" she heard one of the soldiers yell. One of the small boys answered.

"I didn't do anything! Y-you are the one who destroyed my house! Where are my mom and dad?" he said as he cried, tears falling down his face, and his voice constantly muffled by the deep breaths of air he had to take as he wept for his family. Dalia's heart broke just looking at him. He looked scared stiff, and his voice shook and broke every time he spoke. His face looked as if it had so many more years on it than it should have, and his eyes were swollen from crying.

"Oh, really? So you weren't the one who threw the juice carton at me?" the soldier snarled back at him, sarcastically. Then he abruptly grabbed the small boy by his collar. "Listen here. If you don't tell me the truth, you'll get into a large amount of trouble. Understood?"

"But I am t-telling the truth! One of the other boys threw the juice c-carton at you!" the boy answered, trying to free himself from the soldier.

"I gave you your chance," the soldier said, looking at him with scorn. "Take him away to the facility. And bring his brother too," he ordered the men around him, keeping his

The Voiceless Dream

gaze steadily on the boy's timid and fearful one. The boy and his brother were then blindfolded forcefully. The small and helpless children began screaming for their parents, but were pushed away, out of Dalia's sight, as ten men crowded around the small boys as if they were criminals.

Dalia propelled her anger back the way it came; away from her mouth. She forced it all back down her throat. The men who were driving the truck she was still in were talking with the devil of a man who had been threatening the boys. Dalia watched them while her frustration and anger flared like a forest fire all over her. *What if this had happened to him? What if his house was destroyed and his children were about to die? What if he died of fear wondering where they were?* She shifted her gaze away from them and concealed herself once again in the truck.

Dalia sulked alone with these deprecating thoughts until the truck finally began to move again. She watched the village seep away from her sight. She turned her head back and looked at her feet. She took a deep breath, her heart still heavy with despair. She hoped she wouldn't need to see anymore of this torture. Her soul was burdened enough from the fear of her family being killed already, and she felt that if she saw anyone else being treated horribly once more, her soul would collapse with its burden.

Broken. That was all she ever felt. She knew the feeling so well, it felt as if she almost was fated to be with it for eternity. And then there was the principle of patience. It was always said that patience was rewarded. But still, Dalia couldn't help wondering if *all* patience was rewarded. What if her people

The Voiceless Dream

would never get the freedom they had lost back, even after decades of being stripped from it, waiting for it to return? Dalia shuddered with horror and despondence at the thought. She didn't want to despair anymore. She was tired of it.

She looked up and saw that now, the sun was just beginning to peek up from the horizon, with blinding orange light. She looked back behind her, and saw that the village was out of sight; only hilly and rough land, with a few trees and lots of bushes, surrounded her. She picked herself up out of the stacks of cases, and put herself atop of the heap, crossing her legs in front of her as she sat. *I just want to have one day, just one day where I can live. I don't live every day, I just struggle to survive. I wish I could run away from this life. Leave it like it never existed.* Dalia's head became heavy, and her eyelids began to droop. She began to sway.

The truck turned a sharp curve. Dalia quickly became alerted again. She had almost fallen asleep. She slapped herself. *Don't fall asleep, idiot! You're almost there!* The truck's engine hummed in her ears another half-hour longer, until she began to hear voices again.

"Not again. Please let this end," she sighed morosely. The voices became louder. Dalia looked past the truck and saw that once again, they were approaching another settlement. She climbed back down in between the cases. She peeked between them.

The voices were not just voices; they were screams, yells, cries, and pleading. Smoke began to blur her sight a bit, and she heard gunshots everywhere. They were nearing what

THE VOICELESS DREAM

looked like a Palestinian town and outside it, she saw IDF trucks and two large tanks parked in front of the outer buildings. Dalia's heart was immediately in her throat. She tried to breathe, but couldn't. There were so many military vehicles.

The voices were now louder than ever, and soon a crowd with several people holding up her flag. Her identity. Some wore the *keffiyeh*, the traditional checkered scarf. But the protesters were not the only people that caught her eye. She also noticed that there were families moving behind the protestors, at the far end of the crowd. She was able to see them. A grandfather holding a small baby, a father, mother, and daughter, and another father with his son. *They're probably trying to leave for a safer place before this protest turns into chaos,* Dalia realized.

She could feel the tension radiating from the protest. With all the military vehicles, in no time this area would turn into a shooting ground.

In front of the protestors were IDF soldiers and officers blocking their path. Some of them were wearing gas masks. She soon saw why. The officers moved closer to the group and began spraying something at them. *No! What is that?* Then she remembered what her grandfather told her through his tears. *Throughout this Intifada, around two thousand of us have been killed and almost fatally injured, because they have tear gassed us, shot us, and jailed us for our protests for liberation and freedom against their occupation.*

The IDF officers were about to teargas the protestors. And so they did. Dalia watched in complete horror as the

THE VOICELESS DREAM

protestors began to run, only to be caught within the tear gas. The soldiers and officers began throwing a few small bombs of the substance towards the protestors, and several others threw stun grenades. The protesters scattered. Dalia threw her hand over her mouth. She wanted the truck to move but it wouldn't. Dalia peeped her head slightly and saw the men, who had been driving the truck she was in, grabbing masks from a nearby equipment vehicle and helping the other soldiers and officers.

And then her mind reminded her of something. *Wait. Where are the families? Did they make it past here?* Dalia moved between the cases, subtly, and began frantically searching for the families she had seen. Then she heard a cry to her left. She turned her head, and inched closer to the sound. Then she saw them. The father she had seen was screaming over his daughter and wife's bodies. His daughter was coughing, as if she was choked. Her mother was also violently coughing and rubbing at her eyes.

Dalia was about to force herself to turn her gaze away, but in that instant, an IDF soldier began to open fire at the dispersing protestors. Three of them were targeted at the man, his wife, and his daughter, but only two of the bullets struck their target. The girl and her mother both stopped coughing almost simultaneously. The mother's head slumped to the ground, and then her daughter's skull fell beside her mother's head. Only seconds later, they were motionless.

The father's face fell into shock. He looked as if he would fall over any moment. Dalia was unable to look any longer at the sorrowful scene in front of her.

The Voiceless Dream

Only one word tumbled from her mouth. "Why?" Dalia said in dismay, breathing heavily, with tears stinging her eyes. "So then where are the baby and grandfather? Where is the son and his father" Dalia asked aloud, panicked, to no one in particular. She searched and searched, turning her head in every direction and stumbling all over the heaps of cases. They were nowhere to be seen. *Maybe they escaped.*

But soon, Dalia saw she was wrong as her eyes laid onto three figures beside one of the cream-colored apartment buildings to her left. As she strained her eyes through the blurring smoke, she saw that an IDF soldier was kneeling on the old grandfather's neck. The smallest figure was lying motionless on the ground, only a few feet from the old man and the IDF soldier. *No! No! No! No! The elderly man . . . the baby . . . Why? Why? Why! Why can no one here even have a chance to exist?* Dalia shrieked in her head. It was the most gruesome scene she had ever witnessed. She felt as if a black hole had appeared inside of her, sucking all of the oxygen from her lungs.

The truck began to reach the depths of the town, and gradually slowed as other military vehicles began moving around it on the road. Dalia ducked down, lowering her body, but peeked up from the edge of the truck. And in an instant she immediately spotted them up ahead.

There was still a blur of smoke everywhere but she easily spotted the man and his son. They were crouching against the wall of a large building. IDF vehicles were surrounding them. The small boy had his hands over his head, his face hidden by his forearms. His father had one arm around him,

The Voiceless Dream

trying to shield him from all of the mayhem, with his other arm above his head as a sign of surrender.

The father's face had a look of unfiltered alarm and angst all over it, and his son had his eyes shut tightly as he crouched against his father. The little boy's hands slid down to his face as he turned his head away from all of the chaos that was occurring around him. Dalia's tears didn't stop filling her eyes. The sight in front of her, the looks of terror and pain on their faces, it was just all too much. It was unjust. It was immoral. Everything that was being committed against these innocent people caught in this conflict was immoral.

The truck she was in began to approach them, shifting upward occasionally from the uneven road. Almost as if on cue, the IDF soldiers began firing bullets. They were fatal bullets, right from rifles. Dalia threw her hands over her ears but did not bother to duck down, for she was hidden from view on an IDF vehicle; she knew that the soldiers would not fire toward her. The gun shots grew louder and the poor boy and his father were visibly trembling with fear; even with the blur of the smoke, Dalia could see them. They ducked their heads away from the sound of the guns.

And then the world stopped. It paused. Dalia's heart was ripped apart and mauled by the hands of her fear, as a fiendish sight erupted in front of her eyes. Some soldier had fired a shot at the little boy and his father. The little boy suddenly fell in his father's lap, his hands falling away from his face. The father of the child looked down at his son and held him, while saying something to him. The little boy moved his mouth for a second, like he was trying to say

THE VOICELESS DREAM

something back, but then his head fell down, away from sight, as he died in his father's lap. The father looked down at his dead child. His mouth gaped open and his head fell back in shock and terror; his body became limp.

Dalia felt her body tremble, then fall. Her head slammed into the cases beneath her, hard, but she caught a hold of her senses before she fell into unconsciousness. Pushing her horrified form upward, she focused once more on the man and his son. She could see a smear of dark blood on the white wall of the apartment building where the boy had been crouching just seconds ago.

Madness surrounded her. The scream, the explosions, the guns, the voices of death-gripped spirits all twirled beside her. She just couldn't understand how this was all happening at once. Smoke and tear gas were filling the air, and Dalia's vision was growing weaker. She began to cough. The tear gas was entering her; she had to hide away.

Dalia ran her hands over the equipment in the truck until she finally felt an open case beneath her hands. She fit herself into it and shut the lid closed. She coughed once more. When she tried to take a deep breath, her body shook uncontrollably and she felt a tearing pain in her lungs, as if they were being split apart. She put a hand to her chest and clutched the material of her shirt in pain.

Dalia wanted to empty all of her burdens and leave them behind, right where she was, but they would not leave her. Her soul would always have to forever hold the weights of hell that she had been given, ever since she had entered this

THE VOICELESS DREAM

cruel, and hateful world. She felt herself fall away, and allowed her mind to loosen its hold on her senses.

Risks, Risks, Risks

Dalia awoke to a dark, airless atmosphere. She was still in the case, with it pressing hard against her side. She could barely move her head. She felt the band under her fingers and pulled on it, then climbed out and found herself gasping for air. How long had she been asleep?

She tried to maneuver around the equipment surrounding her, but it began to fall from under her. Dalia quickly snatched her hand from the loose pile of cases and sat back. Tilting her head up above her, she saw that the sun was still low in the sky. It was still morning. She probably hadn't been asleep for that long.

The Voiceless Dream

Dalia looked around herself now, and saw buildings and homes lined around her. Not one soul was out on the street. However, these did not match the buildings of a village. They looked different. Some were taller and wider. Dalia quickly climbed down from the pile she was sitting on and hid among the cases.

"We must be here now! I made it!" Dalia whispered with relief, but it was soon gone, as she began to recall the events that had occurred just that morning.

She knew it had not been a dream, for she could still feel the tearing pain in her chest and the strange smell of the tear gas that stung her nose. Her mood became dark, but she tried to change it. She was about to finally find her brother. An image of her grandfather slipped into her head. He was probably searching for them now, scared out of his mind.

Dalia shook her head. "No. Don't think about that now, Dalia. Focus. You need to find your brother first," she told herself sternly. She took one last deep breath, and then hid herself back into her case.

It felt like hours had passed before Dalia felt the truck stop. She began to feel scared, intimidated almost. Her heart climbed up into her throat, and she froze. She was surrounded by people who wanted to kill her, with only a case concealing her. If one thing went wrong, if she made one misled decision, it was game over. She shut her eyes tightly and tensed. Soon, she felt her case being picked up.

The Voiceless Dream

"Woah, when did this equipment get so heavy?" she heard a man ask when he lifted her case. *Are they going to open the case?*

"They never got heavy. You just became weak," she heard someone say. Then she heard muffled snickers. Phew! She was safe, for now. The case swung back and forth slightly as she was carried into the building.

Dalia was trembling uncontrollably. Her skull bumped the case several times. She grew scared that it would be noticeable through the case. A couple of minutes passed, and then she felt the case stop swinging. She felt no movement. Where was she? Then the man carrying her began to move again. Soon she heard keys jingling, a click, and then a door creaking open.

Dalia was flipped upside down as the case was set on the ground. After having to constantly take refuge in a cramped and claustrophobic weapon case, Dalia felt an urge to jump out almost immediately, but she restrained herself and instead tried to keep her ears alert for any alarming signs around her. She heard faint footsteps that seemed to be walking away from her case, and then she heard a door close.

Dalia waited a few moments longer for her own safety, then flipped her case over, and pulled the cord. She swung onto her hands and knees and breathed heavily after the lid had flown open. She lifted her head and looked around herself. She was in a dark room, but she could see the shadows of the other equipment cases all around her, and file cabinets surrounding them. The area beneath the door provided a small source of light.

The Voiceless Dream

"Ok, I have to get out of here. Soon another man will come and put more equipment in here, and then he will find me," Dalia concluded softly to herself. She raised her knees and crouched down, making her way behind the file cabinets. They should keep her hidden long enough if someone walks in. She needed to figure out another plan fast. At any moment someone could discover her, regardless of where she was hiding. Firstly, how was she to get to the cell and find her brother? What could she use? Where were the cells? Maybe she could—

Dalia had no time to finish her thought, because her ears heard the door creak open. Her heart began to skip. She lowered her eyes to the ground. She saw the shadow of a soldier. Her hands became sweaty. She turned her head back slowly and stared at the wall directly in front of her.

Don't do anything stupid! Just wait for him to leave! she ordered herself. But the man didn't leave. He was moving toward the file cabinets. Dalia watched in terror and alarm as the man's looming shadow crept closer. *What should I do? What do I do!* she thought, panicked. His boot was right beside the side of the cabinet now. Dalia's eyes widened at the sight of it, and then she immediately turned herself, moving quietly away from him, around the file cabinet. She paused when she had made it to the other side of the cabinet.

She peeked back around the cabinet and saw again that the man's shadow was unmoving, and the front of his boot also remained motionless. *Why isn't he leaving? What does he want?* And right at that moment he spoke.

THE VOICELESS DREAM

"I know you are in here," he whispered, his voice raspy. Dalia's hands flew to her mouth and her soul gripped her vocal cords in warning, restraining her screams.

Her eyes felt like they would fall out of her head. Her heart was beating so loudly she was scared he would hear it. Maybe he had, for he began moving toward her position again. Dalia fled from where she was hiding, still crouching, but she forgot to be quiet. She cursed herself and then looked up. She could make out the man's figure in the dark, and she could *feel* his gaze on her.

He leapt toward her, and Dalia jumped away from his attack. He collapsed on the ground. She ran and hid behind the nearest file cabinet. *How did he know I was in here? How do I get out of here? Oh, he's going to kill me!*

"I will find you! You can't hide in this room forever!" he yelled into the darkness. Dalia frantically searched around herself. To her right, were only more equipment cases and file cabinets. To her left, was the same thing, except, there was another object as well, hidden among some boxes. She couldn't tell what it was, for it was across the room.

She looked past the cabinet she was hiding behind and caught the man's figure frantically hunting for her among the equipment cases. Dalia looked back at the mystery object, then swiftly and quietly began to make her way toward it, pausing every few seconds to hide behind a cabinet. Finally, she was right beside the object. She could make out its shape better now. It looked like some sort of cart, and it had cloth drapes across its top and sides.

The Voiceless Dream

Dalia hurriedly scanned the room again. Soon, she was able to make out his form. He was scouring for her behind the file cabinets on the opposite side of the room. She ducked into the cart, keeping as quiet as she could. She went into it on her knees, and brought her knees to her chin to fit better when she was settled.

The white cloth hid her, but she didn't know for how long she could hide there. It was only a matter of time before the soldier discovered her location. *I need a way to get out of here! I need a plan! Think Dalia! Think!* Suddenly, she heard the door open again with its heart-dropping creak. More panic strode into her head. Did the man call a friend to help him? Dalia waited for a few seconds in her chilling panic. She began to shake and held her breath, trying to calm herself.

"What are you doing here? And why is the equipment all over the room?" Dalia heard someone ask. This time, the voice seemed to be that of a woman

"There is someone in here!" the man said to the woman, with a heavy breath.

"Nonsense! Who could be in here? We have this facility heavily guarded!" the woman argued.

"But I saw someone! They are hiding in here now! One of the men was carrying a case inside, but I saw the case *shake* on its *own!*" the man retorted back to her.

"That is stupid. You must just be seeing things. Now get back and do your job, or I'm going to have to tell the General you've been slacking off. Move!" the woman commanded him, spitting out the last word.

The Voiceless Dream

Dalia heard his heavy footsteps leave the room. She internally felt a small wave of relief hold her. At least he was gone. Then the woman spoke again.

"Daniel! Get over here! Take this cart and serve the food to the prisoners. It's already nine in the morning!" she called down the hall, her voice now less audible to Dalia.

Dalia felt her chest tighten again. *Wait. Does she mean this cart? Oh, she does! And what food?* Her stomach began to growl. Dalia held it tightly, in an effort to keep it from making any more noise. *Hopefully, she didn't hear that. I haven't eaten in so long,* she thought numbly.

As soon as her stomach stopped rumbling, she felt a push. The cart was moving. Dalia held onto the edges of her seat, or rather, the edges of the metal cart she was sitting inside of. Soon, she saw light spill over the drapes, as the cart left the equipment room. The air felt much cooler here than in the room. She could hear heavy footsteps constantly moving all around her.

The cart's wheels squeaked as they rolled. The sound pierced her ears. The cart stopped, and Dalia felt her stomach drop. *What is going on?* At that moment she heard a ding, and the cart advanced. Soon, Dalia began to smell food. However, it did not smell very pleasant. *Is this really what they give the detainees and the people they jail here? I hope it tastes better than it smells,* Dalia voiced in her head with distaste.

Then the cart entered the kitchen. The air was much warmer here, and Dalia saw many feet, and shadows, move from behind the drape. She heard plates and pots being put on top of the cart. After a few more minutes, Dalia finally felt

THE VOICELESS DREAM

a push, and knew the cart was rolling along once more. It stopped and then her stomach plummeted again, and then a ding much like the first.

She thought throughout the ride, trying to think of any idea to help her get this job done. But what could she do? She was alone, hungry and tired, in a place she could be killed in within minutes. She had been lucky she had escaped the consequence of her last mistake, but she may not be so lucky the next time. Then a scream tore right through her thoughts. She recognized it immediately, and felt excitement fill her head and heart. *Abdul! Abdul!* She was so close to finding him now. He was here, in one of the cells! Abdul! Her brother was here!

The cart stopped, and Dalia waited in anticipation for it to move again, trying to keep herself from jumping out from her concealed position. She heard a door click open, and she heard the man driving the food cart yell into a room.

"Here's your food! Take it quick!" he ordered. Dalia was now being advanced into a room. Her brother was still screaming, but the sound was not close. He was not here. Food was taken from off the cart.

Dalia had the urge to lift up the cloth that hid her just to see what the detainees looked like here. Were they fed enough? Were they tired? But before she could decide whether or not to do that, the food cart turned, and left the room. The cool air of the hallway sent shivers up her spine, but she focused on the screaming. Her brother's cries echoed through the hallway.

The Voiceless Dream

"I better get over there and shut that idiot up!" she heard the man say with a loud growl. Anxiety and excitement flew around her. Her heart beat faster, and she had to restrain herself again from jumping out of the cart and running to find him herself. She was about to see her brother! But hesitation also mixed with her excitement, worrying her at what her brother could look like now. *Please don't tell me they beat him.* The cries became louder, as the cart began to move faster, nearing the sound. *This man must really hate my brother. I hope he doesn't hurt him.*

Abruptly the cart stopped, and Dalia heard the man talking with someone else. *Who is he talking to?* she asked in her head. Then, she heard a door click open and now the cries were much louder. The cart flew into the room, and then stopped and Dalia heard heavy footsteps run past her. The man had moved from the cart. This was her chance.

Dalia lifted up the drape a few inches, and then tilted her head down to look past it. Right in front of her sight was a bed, held up by wooden legs. Dalia looked to her right and saw the man, who had been pushing this cart, looming over a small figure on the ground, who was raising his hand above his head to protect himself.

Focus. she told herself in her head. Dalia lifted the drape up higher, swung her legs out, and then bolted towards the bed. She quickly rolled under it. Dalia slid away from the bed's edges. She jumped slightly when she felt something beneath her shoes. She turned her head hastily and saw that it was Abdul's jacket, the one she had dressed him in barely a

THE VOICELESS DREAM

day ago. The day they had taken him. Dalia forced her gaze away from it.

When she poked her head out slightly from beneath the bed, there were detainees looking right at her. There were two small boys, who looked a bit older than her brother, and three men. They looked so tired, almost as if they were about to fall over. But, looking at her now, they had their eyes wide open. Dalia put a finger to her lips, to tell them to stay quiet about her presence, and then held her hands in a praying motion begging them. The boys and men all nodded their heads at her, and turned their attention away.

Dalia did the same. She hid herself back beneath the bed, her stomach flat on the hard floor. She felt like coughing, but she restrained herself, keeping her hand over her nose and mouth. She finally allowed herself to focus on the man who was still verbally abusing her brother. She didn't want to listen to it, so she allowed her hands to settle over her ears.

Dalia did not know how long she had waited there, attempting to lock out the man's voice from her head, until she finally saw the boots walking away, the door closing behind him. Dalia slowly lowered her hands from her ears and breathed a heavy sigh of relief. She then crawled out from under the bed. As she stood up, she saw that every single person in the cell was looking at her.

"Who are you?" one man asked.

Bitter-Sweet

Dalia froze. She tried to speak but couldn't. She turned her head away from the unfamiliar faces staring at her, and looked instead in Abdul's direction, beginning to walk slowly toward him. He looked horrible. He had bruises all over his face and bare arms, and a cut ran from his temple down his cheek.

"Abdul . . ." Dalia began, her voice breaking, "What did they do to you?" she knelt on the ground, beginning to weep again, and hugged him tightly. He looked up at her, and his eyes widened as he recognized his sister. He hugged her back.

THE VOICELESS DREAM

"You know him?" she heard someone ask. Dalia answered without looking to see who had asked the question "Yes. He is my brother. I hid in an IDF vehicle and moved through the building until I finally found him."

Dalia heard murmurs all around her. "Are you okay?" the same person asked.

"I can't talk now," Dalia replied, her voice suddenly breaking apart like glass.

"Oh, yes. We will wait for you," someone else said. And so Dalia and Abdul were left alone, and sat there, holding each other for a while. Dalia didn't want to know what those horrible soldiers and guards had done to him. She didn't want to think about it. She knew she wouldn't be able to bear the answer. He must have been so scared here. So alone. He must have imagined that everyone had deserted him.

After a bit of time, Dalia sensed her brother was asleep. He was resting his head on her shoulder. She lifted him up and carried him to the closest bed. He was so light. Then she covered him with a blanket. The bed was the exact size as the one her brother slept in at home, but the blanket was slightly thinner. She hoped he wasn't cold.

Dalia turned her head and looked at the detainees sitting on the beds and chairs that were scattered about the room. The cell itself was dim, with no windows in sight. Only two small lanterns on shelves on either side of the room emitted an orange glow.

The Voiceless Dream

A man cleared his throat. Dalia turned to her left and looked at him. He was middle aged with a dark beard and old torn clothing. *They are just like me,* Dalia thought. The man spoke slowly. "Tell us. How did you get here? And how did your brother get here? Sit down, and tell us," he asked her gently, pointing toward a seat in the far corner.

Dalia looked back at him, then made her way toward the seat in the far corner. She picked it up and set it against the far wall, the wall opposite the cell door, where she could see everyone. She sat down, and faced them all. There were a few small boys, older men, and only one other boy who looked about her age.

"My name is Dalia. I am from a small village, at the edge of the Gaza strip. About a day ago, my grandfather told me to take my brother and go to the market area in our village to buy medication for my brother . . ."

Dalia told them all the story of her journey. She told them about how she had to hide in a case with little air, to stay out of sight of the IDF soldiers. She told them about the truck ride and the horrible things she saw. She told them about how she was almost caught by a soldier with a raspy voice while in the equipment room. At hearing about that soldier, all of their eyes grew wide. They glanced at each other. *Do they know him?* she thought with growing curiosity.

When Dalia had finished telling them about her journey there was silence, but it was short lived. All of the detainees and prisoners began asking her many questions; some asked about how she had made the plan with such little time, others asked whether she was ok or not. Dalia noticed that only one

The Voiceless Dream

boy in the room did not ask her anything. He was looking away from her, at the ground. She peeled her gaze away from him, and replied to everyone's statements and concerns, and when it was all over, she walked back over to Abdul's bed, and sat beside it.

Dalia immediately felt a headache and rush of nausea all throughout her body as she sat down. She almost toppled over from it all. As she leaned her head back against the wall, she drew her legs up. Dalia let her head fall down and rest on her knees, *That was too much fear and anxiousness for one day. I almost got killed too many times. Hopefully I can escape this place more easily.*

"Dalia," someone said beside her. Dalia lifted her head slowly, and turned to look at the boy sitting next to her. The same boy who had seemed to ignore her.

"What do you want?" she replied, moving away from him. *When did he get there?* Dalia unconsciously began to examine the boy. He had thick dark hair. His eyes were the color of toffee. He looked tired and his white shirt and black pants had dust in a few places, just like his shoes. Dalia looked down at her own old white shoes. He was sitting in the same position as her, but his head was against the wall behind them.

Dalia spoke cautiously to him. "Who are you?"

The boy, not looking at her, replied with a flat tone. "My name is Inas."

Dalia glanced down at the floor and then back up at him. Inas was sitting only a few feet from where she was. "Nice to meet you. But not really. Why are you sitting here? With me, I mean."

Inas kept his gaze focused ahead of him. "We all know that you aren't planning to stay here for a while. And the other people in this cell are all either too young or old to assist you much. So, I can help you."

Dalia felt suspicion hold her thoughts. *Why does he want to help me all of a sudden?* She eyed him. *Is he serious or joking?* "How exactly could you help me?"

Inas turned and finally locked his gaze with hers. "I've been here for a few months. I could tell you the times the guards are replaced in their shifts, when the food cart comes around, what types of rooms surround us, and a few other things. Now, there are some men in here that have been here much longer than I have. They can provide you with more information and details."

Dalia knitted her brows in thought. She realized she would need help. She had never quite considered how she would leave the facility if she had been able to enter. There were a few plans she could make just from what Inas had told her just now. But they were messily constructed. She turned to him and said, "Ok. But when is the earliest we can figure out a plan?"

"It's most likely almost night time by now, so maybe tomorrow," he replied. He slowly stood up.

Dalia looked skeptical. "How do you know what time it is, inside of this dark cell?"

Inas gave her an exasperated expression. "Like I said, I've been here a while."

THE VOICELESS DREAM

"Right," Dalia whispered, annoyed with herself. She gazed back up at Inas and at that moment a thought flew back into her mind. "Inas?"

Inas swiveled his head to look at her. "Yes?"

"I remember when I was telling you all about my journey here, that when I mentioned the man in the equipment room, all of you looked . . . well, you all glanced at each other. Do you know something about him that I don't?"

His eyes grew wide and he set his mouth into a thin hard line. "Well," he began cautiously, trying to avoid her curious gaze. "That man who you saw in the equipment room is . . . one of the two men guarding this door right now."

Dalia breathed in sharply. *Just my luck. This isn't good.* "What do you mean?" she voiced softly in disbelief and panic. "What if he finds out I'm in here?"

"Relax. I don't think he will. And we'll help you stay protected. But that's not all about the man. You see, there are things that are said about him. Bad things." Inas scratched the back of his head and began staring at the ground.

Dalia eyed him with curiosity as a sickening feeling rose to her chest. "What bad things? What does he do?"

Inas swallowed and continued slowly, still avoiding her eyes. "He has killed a lot of people in the villages and towns he has patrolled. We've heard he slits hands and faces after they die, or after the soldiers are done torturing them. Then he leaves them in a random place to bleed and rot."

Dalia's heart nearly stopped. Her twisted emotions swelled in her chest. Dalia shook her head in frustration, and

THE VOICELESS DREAM

looked back up at Inas. He gazed back at her with concern. "I'm fine," she whispered, and turned her head away.

Inas understood and left. Dalia kept her head down. *The man who killed my parents could be only feet from me. But I need to see his face and hands before I can really be sure. What if the things that were said apply to someone else? Or what if he doesn't have the same marks?* Dalia sighed. This was all too much. Too much was weighing on her heart, and so much of it was almost incomprehensible. *So much* had happened in barely a day, making her extremely exhausted.

Dalia laid onto the cold floor, with her hands beneath her face. Being this close to the ground, she saw many scratches and red specks on the floor. Wait. No. Those weren't just specks. That was blood. Dalia shut her eyes and tried not to think about what she had just seen. She exhaled silently and kept her eyes shut, trying to force sleep onto her flustered head.

A Dark Night

The dim hallway was freezing. The lights flickered. All of the guards were tired, and struggling to keep their posture. Matt looked at Ran beside him. He seemed as if he was still wide awake.

"How are you not tired like the others?" Matt asked him, staring at him with a dubious expression.

"We are going to switch shifts soon and take a break," he responded while fiddling with his rifle. Then he looked back up at Matt in a curious manner. "I still don't understand why you wanted to guard this cell. We could actually be doing something at the patrolling grounds."

The Voiceless Dream

Matt sighed, annoyance heavily emphasized in his tone. "I already told you. We should guard it because there are so many more Palestinians being arrested these days. We need to keep an eye on them."

Ran turned and looked at Matt. "Listen Matt. You are acting awfully stupid. Your head must be broken. Let's leave for the patrolling grounds tomorrow!"

Matt broke his gaze from Ran's and looked down at the ground in thought. Maybe his head was broken, because he did want to leave for the patrolling grounds around the villages and towns. But, nonetheless, he still could not shake off the strange feeling the boy had given him. *I'm probably just sleep deprived,* he thought to himself. He looked back up at Ran.

"Fine," he answered reluctantly.

Ran's face lit up, "Great! See, that's the Matt I know!"

"But . . ." Matt began.

"But what?" Ran questioned him.

"We should take the night patrol. I have some things to do tomorrow," Matt responded.

"You ruin everything," Ran said in exasperation.

"Oh, come on. The night patrol is better than the one in the daytime."

"No, the daytime patrol is better for us."

"No, I still choose the night patrol," Matt replied calmly.

"Find. Your choice," Ran replied with distaste. "But you really are missing out."

The Voiceless Dream

Matt didn't argue back. He shifted his position slightly, and breathed a heavy sigh. Suddenly, a fleeting thought swept into his head. The boy, who he had captured a day or two ago, had stopped screaming, or rather, making any noise. Strange. He glanced at Ran, then hesitantly said, "Hey, Ran?"

"Yeah?" Ran replied distractedly, not looking at him.

"Why has that boy stopped yelling?" he asked. A rapid expression of realization flew over Ran's face, as he turned to look at the cell door behind them.

"I didn't realize that before. He was screaming the whole night last night," he said slowly. Then his expression changed as he shook his head. "Let's just be thankful he shut his mouth. My ears were starting to kill me. We might jinx this if we keep talkin' about it."

"Yeah, you're right," Matt responded. *He probably lost his voice from all of his crying and shrieking,* he thought dismissively. They waited there for only a short time before the guards for the next shift came. Ran and Matt walked off down the hall.

Ran looked at him sideways. "You look like you're spaced out. What are you thinking about? You've been like that for hours."

"It's nothing," Matt responded.

Ran kept examining him. "I know what's bothering you," he said finally. "You just can't wait to get to the patrolling grounds tomorrow. Well, same here."

Matt laughed at the ridiculous comment. The patrolling grounds were the last place he wanted to be now. "Yeah. That's definitely it. You know me so well."

The Voiceless Dream

"Listen," Ran began in a serious tone, "I don't know what's gotten into you lately, but what I do know is that I'm sure that you will forget about whatever's in your head after tomorrow."

"Hopefully," Matt said dismissively. They approached the elevator, and then stepped inside. He pressed a button to send them up. Ran was still talking.

"The General said we'd be able to annex their territory soon," he continued.

"We'll need to move more of them to do that," Matt said, with a nefarious hint in his voice.

"I can't disagree. The more of them that leave, the easier it is for us to take the land back for us," Ran replied. "Finally, after centuries of waiting, we have it back. Now, all we need to do is figure out how to move them off of it."

"*We* are how to move them off of it," Matt whispered to himself. *Centuries of living away from our ancestors' homeland, being persecuted and tortured, and now we can return and restore it. The only thing stopping us is them. The inhabitants.*

Patience

The night sky was filled with shadowed clouds, of which all loomed above the facility. Of course, Dalia couldn't see the sky. As she awoke, the only light she could see was from the two lanterns in the cell. They continued to radiate a dim orange light. She looked around and realized that she was the only one awake. Dalia slowly stood up and looked down at Abdul, still asleep in his bed.

She sat back down and brought her legs up to her chin. *This is probably the only peace and quiet I'll get for a long while.* She sighed. Tomorrow she would need to leave this facility. Or rather, she would need to leave this facility *very soon*.

The Voiceless Dream

Today, she would need to spend time figuring out a plan. She buried her face in her hands.

"Dalia?" someone said in the darkness. Dalia perked her head up. There was a figure moving in the room. Even with the light that the lanterns gave, she couldn't tell who it was.

Who is it?" Dalia responded. The figure came closer and then she was finally able to tell who it was. "Inas. Why are you awake?"

"I should be asking you that," he said as he sat down beside her. "Do you always wake up this early?"

"Why? What time is it?" Dalia asked, startled. *It's morning, right?*

Inas shrugged, "It's probably one in the morning. I don't hear much activity with the guards or anyone else in the building now." He turned his head and gazed at her suspiciously. "What were you doing here awake anyway?"

"Trying to figure out a plan," Dalia replied without looking at him.

"Did you come up with anything?" Inas inquired.

"Maybe I would have if *someone* had given me some information to use."

"Oh. My bad. I thought I could tell you tomorrow, but I can tell you what I know now," Inas offered.

"Ok. Tell me then."

"What do you want to know?" he asked.

"I don't know. Just tell me some of what you know about this place, and I'll see if I can make a strategy from it."

Inas exhaled, then turned his head toward her again and began in a serious tone. "Here are some of the basics then.

THE VOICELESS DREAM

You probably already know this, but I'll tell you anyway. This place is heavily guarded. There are soldiers and guards all around and inside the building. The cells are all on the lowest floor, and there are two shifts for the guards of the cells. One during the day, and one during the night. Two guards stand in front of the door each shift. The way the guards switch shifts—"

"Wait. How do you know all this if you've only been here a few months? It doesn't make any sense," Dalia interrupted.

"I asked the other men in the cell that have been here longer than I have, and I listen and wait every day to find out more," Inas answered. "Now do you want me to continue or not?"

"Fine. Sorry. Continue," Dalia said, rolling her eyes.

Inas continued. "The way the guards switch shifts is they go two by two. The two guards from one cell leave together, and the next guards take their shift when they are gone, and so on. I don't know why they do this. Maybe they think we'll bust out. Anyway, everyday at eight in the morning, 12 in the afternoon, and 10 at night, the food cart comes. The food they give us is like slop and has barely any nutrition. Except for the bread. It may be stale but it's better than the main meal."

Dalia waited, until she thought Inas wouldn't continue. "That's it? That's all you know?"

"No. I know more. I just thought you had a question to ask so I paused," he replied. "It's a lot of information all at once."

The Voiceless Dream

Dalia thought for a second, and then a question hovered into her head. "Is the cell door always locked? Do the guards or soldiers ever come in?"

"Yes the door is locked, and yes, the guards do come in sometimes, but soldiers, no. If you needed to go to the bathroom, or you had some other need, one of them would escort you out, then take you back in. But let me warn you that they wouldn't do it nicely."

"Ok, what else do you know?" Dalia questioned him.

"The soldiers leave for the patrolling grounds in the morning and night. I've even seen them bring dogs with them there." Inas stopped and shivered at the memory. When he spoke, he spoke in a wavering voice. "One last thing. There are equipment rooms and file rooms at the end of the hall, and they are usually always locked. Only a few top ranking soldiers and the interrogation staff have access to them."

Dalia took a deep breath and then returned her gaze to meet his. There was a lot of information to consider. "Is that it?" she asked.

Inas looked like he wanted to say something else, but said instead, "Yes, that's it."

"Ok, so now we need to start creating a strategy to escape," she began. "I think we should leave at night, because my brother will be asleep then, and he won't make any noise."

Inas nodded slowly. "You also can't go back to the food cart. I doubt there'd be enough space for both of you."

"So we need another source of transportation. How should we get out of here?"

THE VOICELESS DREAM

"I think you should find a way to get back to the equipment room," Inas said.

"Good idea. When we get in there, I can try and find cases big enough for both me and Abdul."

"Now the only problem is *how* you'll get to the equipment room," he said.

Dalia wrapped her arms around her legs and thought. She needed to get a key to the equipment room first before she figured out *how* to get there. The keys only belonged to the interrogators, high ranking officers, and soldiers. Dalia tried to force the fatigue away from her head. She brushed her fingers over her hair and felt something. It was her hair clip. A crazy idea flew into her mind. *Well*, she thought bitterly, *it's all I can think of.*

"Inas?" Dalia whispered.

"Yes?" he replied in the same faint voice.

"Do you think the guards that are in front of our cell door are still awake?" she asked him.

He glanced at the door momentarily. "Let's go see." They both stood up and ran to the door quietly. Both pressed their ears to the cold metal door and listened. They didn't hear anything.

"Let's try knocking," Inas suggested.

"Oh, but wait! What if someone wakes up in here?" Dalia whispered frantically.

"Pfft," Inas scoffed. "Everyone here sleeps so heavily at night. Trust me, they won't wake up." Dalia ran to stand in the shadows of a nearby corner as Inas knocked on the door three times. No one answered.

THE VOICELESS DREAM

Dalia ran back over and pulled her hair clip out of her thick hair. Strands of hair fell into her face, and she brushed them away impatiently. She had never tried lock picking before, but she knew how locks operated. She fidgeted with the clip, then felt around with it. She felt an opening between the door and the wall, and stuck the clip in it. She fidgeted again, trying to unlock the door. Inas leaned his head against the door and watched her. After mere seconds had passed, they both heard a click.

Dalia and Inas glanced at each other in surprise as eagerness spread over their faces. Dalia stuck her fingers in between the wall and door and pulled. Inas helped her, and soon the door opened, letting in light from the bright hallway. She peeked outside the door and saw that the guards were slumped on either side of the cell door, sleeping. Dalia put her foot between the door and the wall to keep it from shutting, and then she set her hair clip back where it was, securing her loose hair.

She turned back to Inas. "Ok, here's the plan. We need to find those keys. To do that, we need to sneak through this building and find an interrogator's office."

Inas looked at her with a fearful and demented expression. "You're kidding, right? How are we supposed to sneak through the building? Did you forget what we look like?"

Dalia rolled her eyes impatiently. "No Inas. Of course we can't sneak through the building looking like this. Which is why we will steal their uniforms. "

THE VOICELESS DREAM

Inas eyed her. "You seem a bit small to fit into it, don't you think?"

"I'll just tuck it in and tighten it with the belt."

Inas looked away, smiling, and then began laughing. Dalia kicked his shin and watched as he abruptly stopped, doubling over, and rubbed it in pain.

He looked back up at her with annoyance. "Sorry, but you'll look like a dork if you wear the uniform like that," he said, as he tried not to laugh again.

"I don't care how I look. I just wanna get this done," she sighed. "Now help me out."

And with that, they both quietly stepped out into the hall. Dalia looked down the hallway to either side and noticed that the next cells on either side of them were far enough away that they wouldn't be spotted too easily. The guards in front of those cells were about three meters away, and were either staring straight ahead, or talking to each other. Dalia and Inas both dragged the first guard into the room as quietly as they could. Then they dragged the second guard in. Dalia slipped off one of their boots and set it between the door and the wall again.

She and Inas both stripped off the guards' uniforms and quickly dressed up in them, putting them over their own clothes. Luckily for Dalia, both men were wearing pants and cotton shirts under their uniforms. She sighed with relief. The guns the guards had been carrying had straps, so they both slung them around their shoulders. Dalia tried to fit the uniform on her as best she could, and cursed her slim frame.

THE VOICELESS DREAM

But at least the helmet fit well. She glanced back at Inas. Since he was around a foot taller than her, he fit the uniform easily.

"Now," he began slowly. "Where are we supposed to hide them?" He gestured to the guards still sleeping on the floor.

"Do you think we could take them out of the cell and act like they are detainees?" Dalia suggested.

"I don't know. I am sure they'll wake up. We'll have to knock them unconscious."

"How?"

"I'm not sure either, but I'll try," Inas replied. He ran his hands over the legs of his uniform and from it he pulled out a knife. He hesitantly lowered himself and turned the knife so that the hilt was away from his body. Inas lifted the head of the first guard and rammed the hilt against the back of his head. The guard did not awaken, so he did the same to the second guard.

"Are they still breathing?" Dalia whispered.

"Yes," Inas responded, placing his head near each of their faces. He placed a hand over their chests. "Still breathing and alive."

"I think now we should be able to take them out of this cell and act like they are the prisoners," Dalia suggested.

"I guess it's the only choice that we've got," Inas agreed, shrugging. "But first let's rough them up a little, try to make them look like us."

Dalia nodded, and knelt down onto the ground beside them. She began searching the many pockets of her uniform, and found a knife in one of the leg pockets. With it, she tore a few holes into their shirts, and then Inas knelt beside her and

The Voiceless Dream

hauled up the first man to his feet, with his head slumped to the side.

Dalia slipped the boot beside the door onto her foot, and let Inas walk out of the cell half dragging and carrying the guard. Dalia followed with the second man, but left the knife between the door and the wall so that she and Inas didn't get locked out.

"If anyone talks to us, you do the talking, " she whispered to him. "I know I may not be able to think fast enough to respond."

"Okay," he answered, as they approached a set of guards. "But we should also try and block the faces of these guys too, so they don't recognize them. Keep your head down."

They both shifted their positions and continued down the hall. No one so far had questioned them. Dalia was very worried, however. She was tired of almost getting caught and killed, and she wanted to be more careful, but it was very difficult to do so; danger would always follow her. *What's worse is that now I've dragged Inas into this too. He didn't have to help me, but he did anyway.* But she knew she didn't have time to think about that. She needed to focus on finding a set of keys now. After a few more minutes of heaving, they finally neared the elevator. There were still cells and guards lined behind them.

"Let's get in here," Inas whispered, nodding toward the elevator. They both took a few more heavy steps, and finally entered the inside of it. Dalia forced herself to keep the man she was holding up on his feet, as Inas walked over, easily carrying the other guard, to the buttons of the elevator, and

THE VOICELESS DREAM

pressed something. As soon as the doors closed Dalia slowly lowered the man on the floor and slid slowly onto the ground, panting. Inas soon did the same.

Inas leaned his head against the wall, and crossed one leg behind the other, "Really? You couldn't hold him up just a little bit longer?" he criticized.

Dalia glared at him. "I don't do this everyday, and besides, you look tired too," she added as she began standing up. "This thing is gonna open soon, and we need to pick them up again," she continued, without looking at him.

Inas gave her an irritated glance and heaved one of the men up, slinging his arm across his shoulders. Dalia did the same. At that instant, the elevator opened. They walked out into a hall. This one had much more light, and it began to hurt Dalia's eyes looking into it. There were no cells, and only a few soldiers and officers passed by, barely even glancing in their direction.

Inas and Dalia turned right and walked down the hall. Dalia frantically searched for a place they could get rid of the men. Her arms were keeping them up with difficulty, and she was trying to keep her breathing and panting as subtle as she could.

She diverted her attention back in front of her and saw that up ahead, a man was dragging a cart carrying a mop, broom, and some other supplies in what looked like bottles. She glanced at Inas and saw that he had also spotted him too.

"Follow him," he said roughly to her. "Those cleaning men always have a closet or area to store their equipment."

The Voiceless Dream

Dalia wanted to ask how he knew that, but she was too out of breath to say anything.

She and Inas tried to quicken their pace and followed the man down the hall. After a few minutes, the old, hunched man stopped in front of a door. He didn't even try to pull out any keys. All he did was open the door and push the cart of cleaning supplies past it. He then shut the door and left.

When the man had turned a corner at the end of the hallway and was finally out of sight, Inas and Dalia made their way over to the door. Dalia turned the door knob and opened the door slowly. She looked inside. The cart was still there, and the closet looked big enough for both the guards to fit into. There were mops and brooms hung on the walls, along with other supplies.

"Finally, we can rest our arms," Inas huffed, as he walked past her and lowered the guard down onto the ground. He slumped him against the wall. Dalia did the same.

"We need to hurry!" she urged.

"Agreed," Inas nodded. They both walked out of the closet and Dalia shut the door. Who knew when those guards would wake up, or when someone realized no one was guarding their cell? The faster this got finished, the better.

"Now where do you think the keys might be?" Inas asked her.

"First of all, what floor are we on? I only know that we aren't on the bottom floor anymore."

"We are on the uppermost floor. I remember when I came here for the first time. This was the first part of the building I saw."

The Voiceless Dream

"Do you think the interrogators offices are up here?" Dalia asked quickly. Inas didn't answer, and an uncertain look spread over his face.

Dalia began to glance around. She walked away from Inas. Along the hallway were a few doors to her right. She headed toward them, with Inas at her heels. As she approached the first of the doors, she saw that there were labels beside them. The one in front of her read: Office of the General. *Ok, so this is not an interrogator's office, but this is an office. Inas said that when he first came here, this floor was the first thing he saw. They must have blindfolded him, just as they did to my brother. But why was he up here first?*

"Inas?" Dalia turned her head and looked at him. "Why did they take you up here first?"

She saw his light brown eyes darken fleetingly. "They interrogated me here," he replied. "But why do you want to know that?"

Dalia felt heart rate increase. *Did they do that to my brother too?* Then she stopped herself, regaining control of her thoughts. *Ok, so he said he was questioned here, and there is an "Office of the General" as well, so the interrogator's office must be on this floor too. But where?* She walked down the hall to the next door. The label beside it read: Inspector Dorit.

"Are you going to tell me what you are thinking about or not?" Inas asked her impatiently.

"Just wait," she commanded absently, shaking her head. *This must be the inspector's office, so the offices must all be down this hall.* Dalia briefly looked at Inas and said, "This way."

The Voiceless Dream

He stared after her in bewilderment, and then began following her as she walked down the hall. "So you figured it out?"

"I hope so," she responded, as they both raced down the corridor. *These boots are so large. I wish I could move faster.*

"That's *it*? You *hope* you figured this out?" Inas hissed in her ear with perplexity. "I would like to remind you that we knocked two guards unconscious, stole their uniforms, and are now trying to find a key in a building where we could easily be shot dead on sight if anyone can recognize us."

"Firstly, *you* knocked two guards unconscious. And they wouldn't shoot us *immediately*. They would just interrogate us, Inas."

"Sure. In your dreams. One second they'll tell me to put my hands up, and the next I'll have two 'warning' shots in my back."

"Just trust me. I promise I'll get us through this," she replied, glancing at him. Focusing on the hall again, she realized it would soon end. It turned left. They followed it in that direction. The first door was to her right. She made her way toward it. It's sign read: Interrogator Itan.

Danger, Danger

"We're here," Dalia said to Inas. "Look at the label."

"I see it, but how did you solve this?" he asked dumbfounded, a hint of respect in his tone.

"I'm obviously the smarter one," she replied.

Inas exhaled very audibly, clearly meaning for her to hear it well. "If you're the smarter one, then I'm the better-looking one."

"You don't get to decide that!" she whispered back, turning to glare at him.

"Ah, the jealousy."

"Do you have a death wish?"

"I should be the one asking you that."

The Voiceless Dream

Dalia shut her eyes and then opened them to stare right at him, speaking with a strained voice, trying her best not to argue. "We don't have time for this. Let's just get this over with."

Ins shrugged. "You started it."

Dalia turned her attention back to the office door, biting her tongue to keep herself from yelling at him. She put her hand on the door handle but Inas grabbed her arm before she could push the door open. Dalia looked back at him, scowling"Wait," he whispered. "What if there's someone inside the office? I thought we were avoiding other people in the building."

"Just make up something to get them out of the office then." When Inas still looked uncertain, she said, "I've thought this through . . . " then added in her head, *mostly*. Inas put his hand back at his side, looking uneasily at the office door.

Dalia gazed back at the door handle, pulled down on it, and pushed. The door opened, and inside a man was sitting down at a desk across from where they were standing. He was fully bald, and his eyes looked sharp and bulging. He did not seem friendly at all. Dalia felt a sickening wave fly over her chest, and her hands became sweaty. His head perked up when they came into the room. Dalia glanced at Inas nervously.

"What are you two doing here?" the bald man asked.

The Voiceless Dream

Inas answered in a serious and composed tone, straightening himself slightly. "We were told to inform you that the General would like to speak to you."

The interrogator looked at them in puzzlement. "At this time of night?

"Affirmative," Inas replied, trying to keep his gaze steady with his.

The interrogator hesitantly got up, nodding. "Very well. Where is he?"

Inas blanked, but fortunately, Dalia responded this time. "He is waiting for you outside the building, at the farthest vehicle lot," she said, trying to make her voice as informative and formal as she could.

The interrogator looked even more confused. "How strange. Why would he want to talk to me there?" He began to walk out of the room, but as he did so, he paused and gave both Inas and Dalia a measured look. Dalia held her breath until he finally continued out. They waited until he had turned the corner of the hall to shut the door.

Inas turned to her. "Why did you say the farthest vehicle lot?"

"Well, because it seemed like the farthest place from here," she responded. "Anyway, let's find those keys before he finds out that we lied to him!" They began to hunt for the keys.

The office had in it two file cabinets and a desk with many papers and drawers. It was gray and dreary. Dalia began searching the desk and Inas went to examine the contents of the file cabinets. The desk had many large stacks of paper,

The Voiceless Dream

files, and stamps and was extremely messy. Dalia decided to search the drawers first. Inside of them were paper clips, a stapler, a stack of blank paper, and pencils. She rummaged through each of the drawers as fast as she could, but saw no sign of any key.

"I didn't see a key around or inside the cabinets," Inas told her, walking over to the desk.

"I still need to search the top of his desk," she sighed. She looked up at Inas. "Help me look for it here."

"Ok then, come on," he replied. Both of them moved the stacks of paper off the metal desk and onto the floor. They searched underneath where the paper had been, under and around his computer, and everywhere else atop the desk they could. Dalia felt like melting down.

She fell to the ground in panic and anger, shutting her eyes tightly. She opened them again and there in front of her, underneath the desk was a set of keys, all hooked together. Her eyes widened, as she slowly grabbed them, and stood up, still staring at them with wide eyes as her anger and fear fell away. *I doubt this type of luck will ever come by me again.*

Inas was staring with disbelief at the keys she was holding in her hand. "Finally, you found them! Now let's get out of here! That guy will be back any moment!" Dalia didn't need to be told twice. She stuffed the keys inside one of her pockets and ran out the door, with Inas right behind her. They turned the corner of the hall sharply and continued down it.

"What do we do now?" he asked her, as they ran.

The Voiceless Dream

"Umm . . . " Dalia began, as she thought hard for what to do next.

"YOU DON'T KNOW?"

"Shhh! Someone will hear us! And yes I do know. First we need to test these keys, and figure out which one is meant for the equipment room." She paused as they reached the elevator. Inas opened it for them.

"Then what?" he questioned, as they stepped inside. He impatiently pressed another command for the elevator.

"Then . . . we will come back up here, carry the real guards back down into the cell, dress them in their uniforms, put them back outside the cell, and shut the door." She paused again and her expression became a worried one. "But—"

"But what?" Inas demanded, as he knit his eyebrows at her.

"What if they wake up?" she asked timidly.

"They've stayed unconscious this long. I think they can keep it up a bit longer." He leaned his back against the wall and breathed out. "How long do you think he'll be out there?"

"I don't know."

Inas pursed his lips and nodded. They both waited in anticipated silence as the elevator lowered down. The second the doors had slid open, Dalia and Inas bolted out.

After a few quick minutes, they finally reached the equipment room. Dalia felt a shiver over her spine. She still felt anxious. Nonetheless, she stopped in front of the door and pulled the keys out of her pocket. She inserted the first key into the lock on the door, and twisted it around. It didn't

THE VOICELESS DREAM

budge. She looked down at the chain of keys. There were most likely about 20 more keys to try. More panic and frustration flooded over her as she began to pull out the next key.

Dalia pulled out another key once again. She was trying to work as fast as she could. Sooner or later the interrogator would come looking for them. Not to mention, someone could find the guards that they left in the closet.

"Hurry!" Inas voiced urgently. "It feels as if we've been here for hours!"

"I'm almost done! There are only three more keys to try, unless this one works," Dalia replied in the same impatient tone. She stuck the key into the lock and fiddled around with it. She twisted it left and right, but it didn't budge.

"Ugh!" Inas murmured in exasperation, as he watched her release it. He slammed his hand against the wall beside him.

Dalia disregarded his attitude, pulling out another key. This one was smaller than the last. She tested it, and finally, the door clicked open. Inas and Dalia glanced at each other. Dalia looked down at the key and studied it as quickly as she could. It was a much more vibrant bronze color than the rest, and it was smaller than most of the other keys. Dalia scratched it and left a silver trail on its surface as the bronze color peeled away.

"Why did you do that?" Inas asked her.

"I was marking it so that it will be easier to tell it apart from the other keys," she replied. "Come on! We need to leave. Now!" she whispered. She shut the door of the equipment room silently, and ran off back the way they came.

Dalia wanted this night to be over so badly. She was so close to getting this job done. All she had to do now was move those guards back to their places. *It'll be over soon. I just need to get this part done. I'm so close. I'll get my brother out of here. We'll get back home, and I'll never step foot outside of my home again.*

After several moments of sprinting, they finally made it to the elevator. Once Inas had opened it for them, they stepped inside. Dalia commanded the elevator to rise this time. However, both of them were silent as the elevator rode up. It seemed like time had slowed as they waited inside of it. Inas stood with his arms crossed staring at the ground, and Dalia leaned against the wall, staring at the doors.

Just then, the elevator made a *ding*, and the doors slid open slowly. Inas stepped out first. He began to turn his body to the right side of the hall, but to Dalia's surprise and sudden dread, he stopped dead in his tracks, staring down the hallway.

"What is it?" Dalia whispered, walking out of the elevator towards him. The doors shut behind her. She looked down the hallway at what he was looking at and almost felt her heart stop. Her eyes widened with fear and panic crashed over her soul. There, ahead of them, the interrogator was talking to the two guards they had left in the closet. The guards that were supposed to be in front of their cell, who's uniforms were on *them*.

THE VOICELESS DREAM

"Inas," Dalia whispered, pulling his arm frantically. "We need to get back into the elevator now!"

Inas immediately moved from his place and turned towards the elevator buttons. He pressed at the lower button several times, clearly distraught. The interrogator or the guards could turn their attention towards them at any second, and immediately notice them there, standing in the middle of the corridor. Their sharp gazes could easily shift and spot them both. Death awaited.

Dalia wanted to melt into the ground more than anything. She wanted to disintegrate into a speck of dust and become the most invisible thing existing in the world at that moment. Suddenly, what she had dreaded, happened.

The interrogator turned his head in their direction, doing a double take when he noticed them. Dalia watched in horror as realization slowly spread over his face. He had *recognized them*. The elevator doors slid open, and Inas and Dalia pushed past them and threw themselves into the elevator. Inas fell onto the floor of the machine and Dalia desperately pressed at the elevator controls as she heard the interrogator and the guards yelling after them, their voices growing closer. She stopped when the doors had slid fully shut.

"They are going to catch us any second!" Inas yelled at her. "What do we do? They'll kill us!"

"I know! I know!" Dalia shouted back. She threw her hands on her head in frustration. *Great. Just when I thought things were going to get better.*

"Do you have an idea?" Inas asked her. "Because these doors will open any second now!"

The Voiceless Dream

"Would you stop it! Help me think of something!" Dalia snapped at him.

She put her hands over her eyes and tried to think as hard as she could.

"Ok, so there are two guards and an interrogator that are about to catch us," she said, thinking aloud. "We are still wearing their uniforms, so what can we do? We need to get rid of the uniforms and get back into the cell."

The doors of the elevator slid open in front of them. Inas glanced at Dalia with alarm. "Let's just leave these uniforms outside of the cell, and pretend to be asleep instead," he suggested as they ran out as fast as they could out of sheer fear. The guards in front of the other doors paid no attention to them.

"We can't just leave them outside of the cell! They'll think that whoever did it was in there!" Dalia whispered angrily at him.

"Not unless we shut the cell door. That thing is impossible to unlock, probably because it has no handle from the inside. The only reason we got out here is because of your hair clip," he responded.

"Fine," Dalia reluctantly agreed, as they began to near their cell. She hated the risk of the idea but then again, hadn't the whole plan been the definition of risk itself?

They had just approached the cell when they heard the *ding* of the elevator. Dalia and Inas both froze from the growing terror coursing through their veins and turned to look back down the hall. The interrogator and the two guards were charging right at them.

Better Watch Out

Inas and Dalia let their instincts guide them and immediately sprinted down the hall ahead of them. Dalia knew that the military boots would slow her so she paused and stripped them off, along with her socks. The interrogator and guards were only yards away from her before she had raced back down the hall after Inas. He had not stopped for her, and now he was much farther ahead.

"They found us!" Dalia yelled to him as they ran.

"Oh really? I couldn't tell, Sherlock!" he yelled back.

The Voiceless Dream

Dalia quickened her pace, feeling panic heat her face, and caught the glances of baffled guards in front of the cell doors she passed on her right. The hall was getting darker and the few lights left kept flickering.

"After them!" she heard the interrogator command the guards.

Dalia had finally matched her pace with Inas's. They both were breathing heavily from the run but did not slow. The damp stone corridor continued forward but then twisted to the right. She and Inas propelled themselves forward into the turn, nearly falling off balance. It twisted again and again, and Dalia grew dizzy from the turns. She lost count of them. Her ankles were painfully sore and her gun kept hitting her back.

Dalia could hear several heavy footsteps following their trail, and she could distinctly tell they were still a bit farther off. She and Inas had been faster. But the guards could easily catch up and shoot at any minute if commanded. The only thing stopping them was the winding hall.

The hall finally stopped materializing cells and guards, and now revealed two paths about five yards away. One led to the left, and the other in front of them led downwards towards a staircase.

Dalia knew that if they took the left hall, their pursuers would either corner them or open fire at them, for there would be no place to hide. But if they took the staircase, it would be harder for the guards to catch their victims. Inas was a little ahead of Dalia. The staircase was only feet away.

The Voiceless Dream

Dalia ran up behind Inas and pushed him towards the staircase, but not too roughly. He understood, and then jumped several feet down into it. He didn't fall, but instead caught his footing with agility and continued to sprint down it, skipping about two steps each pace.

Dalia followed his example. She jumped over about seven steps, before she gripped the metal railing, swung her body upward, and slid down it nearly at a full handstand. She could feel the smooth metal heating her hands rapidly. She swung herself down from it as slowly as she could when the staircase began to twist in different directions, taking the railing with it.

She finally landed onto the steps and continued to run. Inas was right behind her. The staircase was leading so far down that there soon was barely a ray of visible light. Dalia and Inas found it harder to keep track of the endless steps, but luckily they could no longer hear any guards in pursuit.

Finally, the steps ended. Dalia nearly tripped, but quickly regained her footing. She and Inas both halted almost simultaneously, holding their breath, and listened to their eerily dark surroundings for several moments. Dalia was the first to break the silence. She released the suffocating breath she had held in her chest. Inas did likewise.

"What do we do now?" he asked, panting. "They'll trace us back to the cell and see our shoes that we left at the door, and then everyone in that cell will be punished!" he finished in a whisper.

Dalia looked up at him. She could barely see him, but could just make out his figure. "I know. This all went so

THE VOICELESS DREAM

wrong." She sighed. "If they end up blaming it on any of the other prisoners, I'll turn myself in. I can't let everyone else pay for my mistake."

"What?" Inas exclaimed in a whisper. "You can't do that! We didn't go through all of this for nothing!"

"We'll just have to wait and see what happens. For now, in case they trace us back to these stairs, let's find a place to hide," Dalia replied.

Inas did not answer her immediately. He only stared at the ground. Eventually he said, "Ok."

Dalia began to walk forward, putting her hands in front of her so that she did not run into anything. Inas followed her. She could just barely see her hand in front of her. After only a few paces, she felt a rough surface beneath her fingers. Wood. She ran her fingers down the surface farther and felt a knob. Inas was still breathing heavily beside her.

"Inas. I found a door," she whispered.

"Open it," he said.

She did. She turned the knob slowly and pushed the door open. Despite its weathered exterior, it didn't creak at all. Inside, Dalia was relieved to see a small black lantern on the floor to her right. It illuminated a small glow, and from it she saw that, just a few feet behind the lantern, there were metal bars.

Dalia's heart skipped several beats. *Why are there metal bars here? Is there a prisoner? Or is it something else?* Inas walked past her and slowly lowered himself to the ground against the wall. Dalia swallowed and shut the door quietly behind her. She sat down beside him.

The Voiceless Dream

"How long until we need to go back up there?" he asked.

"I don't know," Dalia replied with despair. "Maybe about five minutes? We can't stay here long." Her mind began to drift into unrealistic thoughts about the limitless horrors that could be hidden behind the bars.

Inas unstrapped his helmet and set it on the stone floor beside him. Both of them remained silent for a while.

Inas sighed, then looked over at Dalia. "Do you miss your parents?" he asked quietly.

Dalia was thrown off by the question. She averted her gaze to the ground and answered him, trying to keep her voice steady. "Of course I do."

"I wish I could see mine again."

"At least you remember what they looked like. I would love to know what mine looked like."

"Do you have any memories of them?"

"No. I only remember their voices."

Inas turned his head and gazed at the floor wistfully. "So are you and your brother all alone?"

"No, we have our grandfather."

He paused again for a moment. "You're lucky you can leave this cell so soon."

Dalia smiled faintly. "Well, I did leave the cell . . . but I'm still trapped."

"I noticed."

"Do you miss your parents?" she asked him.

"Yes. Very much."

"Do you have any siblings?" she pondered, tilting her head while looking at him.

The Voiceless Dream

Inas swallowed as a hurt expression spread over his face. "I had one little sister, but now she's gone."

Dalia almost instinctively averted her gaze from his face. It had looked so . . . lost. Tormented, as if all of his pain had resurfaced and was stuck in his expression. She looked back at him. She let out her question in a small breath. "She died?"

He did not offer any response at first, but he finally nodded once after several moments.

Dalia felt dismayed. She couldn't imagine what she would do if her brother died. She decided not to press him further about his sister's death. "How did you get here, Inas?"

"I tried to save her, I tried to do something for her, but I couldn't. They took me away and now I'll be locked in the cell for months."

"Do you know where you will go when you are let out of this prison?" Dalia whispered, staring at the ground.

"No. I have nowhere to go. They destroyed my home, and threw me in here. I lost my parents. I'm all alone." He sighed deeply and put his face in one of his hands.

Dalia forced herself to keep her tears away. Inas had no one.

"Dalia."

Dalia looked back up at him. He was staring straight ahead, and she could see a small illumination of the light of the lantern in his eyes.

"When will it all be over? I feel so dead and lifeless after all of the fighting we have to do just to survive. I'm tired of always losing everything. I'm scared that sooner or later, none of us will exist."

The Voiceless Dream

"We might exist, but without an identity."

"I can't imagine that."

"Do you have friends?"

"Yes. They aren't Palestinian, but they are both amazing people."

Dalia tore her gaze away from him. *They aren't Palestinian? Well, if they're Israeli, then I guess I have no problem with that. Inas seemed to think they were good people.* She lifted her knees and brought them nearly in level with her neck. *I shouldn't ask him about his personal life. It could trigger him.* "Do you ever wonder what a normal life is like?"

"A normal life? You mean the one where we have freedom?"

"Exactly."

"I doubt we'll be living that anytime soon."

"Maybe not."

"But at least we have resilience."

Dalia nodded. "At least we have that."

There was a fleeting moment of silence between them again, until Inas spoke again, still whispering. "By the way, why are there metal bars over there?"

Dalia looked over at him and saw the clear fear in his eyes. His pain and sadness had nearly disintegrated from his expression. "I have no idea why," she answered quietly, glancing back at the dark shadows that stayed suspended behind the bars.

"Dalia," Inas whispered. "We have to leave now!"

THE VOICELESS DREAM

Dalia began to feel frantic. She was startled by the rising tension and terror in his voice. "Why?" she asked in one quiet breath.

"The *dogs*. The large dogs they bring to hunt for us are behind those bars," he breathed quietly, his eyes widening with each word he spoke to her.

Dalia felt her throat close. She looked away from Inas and began to stand up. Inas stood with her, snatching his helmet and strapping it on, all in one motion. Dalia quickly tiptoed back towards the door in a few paces with long strides. She quietly turned the knob and opened the door. But just as she did so, she heard a low growl. Inas's eyes widened and he and Dalia both turned their heads to stare right back at a massive black dog facing them. In the darkness, it looked like a bear to Dalia. It bared its bright teeth menacingly and its eyes were in angry slits.

Dalia quickly ran out the door and Inas swiftly left as well, shutting the door behind them as quietly as he could. Dalia felt her mouth fall open slightly. She couldn't feel her breath escape her lips any longer. Inas moved toward the stairs, and Dalia followed, not wanting to be anywhere near the large canines.

"Do you think they didn't follow us down here because of the dogs?" Dalia whispered.

"Maybe," he whispered back. "That dog could have easily begun barking, giving away where we were." They quickened their pace.

THE VOICELESS DREAM

When they finally neared the top, they crouched onto the metal steps and listened. They heard nothing. That could only mean two things.

"Either the guards are still looking for us down the other halls, or they already made it back to the cell," Dalia said faintly, but loud enough for Inas to hear her. She could feel her hands shaking violently from her rising panic. She pressed them harder against the rough surface of the stairs.

"We were only down there for a few minutes. If they were worried enough about us, they would have issued an emergency announcement over the speakers," Inas explained.

"Let's go back to the cell and see what's happened," Dalia offered.

"And if the guards are there?" Inas inquired.

"I turn myself in, and you hide away until it's safe for you to enter the cell," Dalia answered.

Inas gave no argument. They both raised their bodies slowly, barely moving their heads, then finally finished the staircase to the top. With their hearts in their throats, they glanced down the hall to their right. Not one soul was in it. They sprinted forward. Dalia had just become aware of how cold the floor was on her bare feet. It felt like she was running on ice.

They went through the winding halls as quietly as they could. When they began to catch sight of the cell doors, they nearly stopped.

"Dalia, let's slow down our pace," Inas told her. "You walk on my right so they won't see your bare feet. Let's both unstrap our guns and keep our heads down. Got it?"

The Voiceless Dream

"Yes," she responded. They both unstrapped their long guns, and Dalia took her place beside Inas at his right. They lowered their heads and walked forward.

Dalia watched Inas's boots, trying to keep her feet in pace with his long strides. She didn't hear any of the other guards move or speak. After several moments, she allowed herself to lift her head a bit higher. Up ahead, she saw their cell door. It was still unguarded, and every other cell within about 20 yards of it on either side remained without a guard as well.

Just as there were only a few paces between them and the cell, Inas extended his arm in front of her, indicating for her to halt.

"Wait," he said, his voice careful. "Something isn't right."

"Inas, what are you saying? There's no one around the door," Dalia breathed, becoming more frightened from his tone.

"Dalia, I think we're being watched."

Death's Stare

"What?"

Inas quickly glanced behind himself, then gave her a serious stare. "Don't you dare look now, but three of the guards behind us are staring our way. We can get back here later."

Dalia swallowed and walked onward, past their cell. Inas followed right behind her.

"When can we get back here?" Dalia asked him, forcing herself to resist the urge to look back. "Where will we go?"

"Let's climb onto the elevator," he suggested.

"Why? Why not hide in a room?

"We will, but first we need to outdistance our pursuers," he told her, his voice uneven.

THE VOICELESS DREAM

Dalia suddenly realized she couldn't feel her hands any longer. She glanced down for a split second and saw that she had been clutching her gun so tightly that her hands had become extremely pale. She couldn't loosen her hold on the weapon. She was in too much shock. *Will we ever escape this?* Her mind flashed an image of her body strapped to a chair, bleeding.

"Dalia?" Inas said, bringing her back to reality. "Focus. You're not matching your pace."

Dalia obeyed and quickened her pace, feeling more and more nauseous with each step she took. The rest of the walk to the elevator passed by in a quick blur. Once the elevator doors had slid shut, Dalia couldn't contain her frustration any longer. She flung her weapon onto the floor.

"Where are we going?" she yelled at him. "Inas, they'll catch us easier this way! Why do we have to take the elevator?"

Inas raised his hands and answered her slowly. "Calm down. We need to outrun them."

"That makes no sense!" she shot back, her anger growing. "Why can't we stay on the same floor and outrun them, or hide away in a room until they give up?"

"Dalia, we can't go back there with those men watching us! We have to keep our distance and then return."

Dalia sighed and tilted her head upward. She caught a glimpse of a loose tile on the elevator's ceiling above her. "Where are we going?" she asked again, her voice more composed.

The Voiceless Dream

Inas was never given the chance to answer her, because at that moment, the elevator shook violently, and its lights flickered.

"Inas?" Dalia called, putting a hand to the wall. Her stomach felt as if it had been folded inside-out. Her chest was choked by her panic and she could feel the walls of the elevator shaking beneath her hand. Inas gazed back at her with the same demented expression she was giving him.

The elevator shook harder, and Dalia's legs collapsed beneath her. The elevator went dark.

"Inas?" Dalia called again, sprawled on the floor. "Where are you?" She felt like crying.

No response came.

"Inas?"

Nobody replied.

"Inas, answer me!" she yelled again.

Still no response.

Dalia began to move backwards until her spine hit the wall of the machine. *What happened to him? Where is he?* Her breathing was awfully loud and barely controllable. The darkness was beginning to intimidate her. It was nearly pitch-black.

"Dalia?"

Dalia flinched, then felt a slight twinge of ease. "Inas? Where are you?"

"Ah . . . " he groaned. "I hit my head."

Dalia heard him sit up. She couldn't see him at all.

"The elevator stopped working," he told her in a haggard voice.

The Voiceless Dream

"What do we do?"

"I don't know."

Dalia wiped at her eyes. They were damp. Tears must have escaped her eyes without her realizing it. She released a ragged breath and became more conscious of her aching head. It felt like someone was attempting to pull all of her nerves out from it.

"We need to get out of here," Inas muttered.

Dalia didn't answer. She shut her eyes and her deprecating thoughts began to tug at her. *How are we supposed to escape? There's nothing here. Nothing.* She lifted her eyelids and closed them again. *Of all the places to be, I'm stuck in an elevator with a group of angry authorities chasing me.* Images of the elevator flickered past her eyes. A fragment of mercy pried its way into an image.

"Inas," Dalia whispered, wanting to cry out from the growing triumph she felt.

"Yeah?"

"I think I have an idea."

Dalia rammed her weapon into the tile on the elevator's ceiling again again. Past it, she knew, would be the elevator shaft. If they could climb it, there was a possibility they could escape.

"I think it's gonna fall off soon," Inas commented. He swung his arm upward and his gun collided with the tile again. They both heard it swinging. After a small number of seconds, the shaft's opening plummeted right at Inas's head.

THE VOICELESS DREAM

"Ow!" he grimaced, as his helmet transmitted the vibrations from the impact. The large tile was on the floor beside his feet.

"Focus Inas. Now, you know what to do, right?"

"Yeah," he affirmed, touching the top of his military helmet. He looked above at the opening in the ceiling and knelt beneath it. He bent his arms and overlapped his hands.

Dalia ran backwards, counting her footsteps until she hit the wall behind her. *This had better work*. She bolted forward. *One, two, three!* As her head called out the last pace, she suddenly felt a less stable surface beneath her foot. Nevertheless, she used her speed and energy to propel herself upward. She kept her hands and arms out in front of her and instinctively gripped the edge of the shaft's opening the moment she had felt it beneath her fingers.

"Did you make it?" he asked.

"Yes!" Dalia responded, lifting her body and dragging herself into the shaft. She sat up and found herself at the very top of the elevator.

It was bright enough for her to see the gears and other mechanical objects and wiring settled on the elevator's surface. She decided not to let her eyes stray to the long drop beneath her. Her nerves were busy enough managing the fear she already had. Looking up, she saw cords, tubes, thin bars, and electric boxes spaced out on the four tall walls surrounding her. The length of the shaft disappeared into an intimidating darkness looming above her. But right before the dark met the feeble light of the large shaft, on the left wall, there was an open vent.

The Voiceless Dream

"Hey! Get me up there!" Inas demanded, startling her. His voice echoed throughout the shaft.

Dalia forced herself to near the elevator's opening again. Now that her eyes had adjusted to the darkness, she was able to just barely recognize his figure. She dangled her arm and after a few moments, Inas's hand was grasping it. Dalia pulled upward, her other arm and hand using the floor to steady herself.

She continued to pull, but then the force on her arm eased slightly. Inas's hand was now clenching the edge of the opening. Dalia hauled him upward, and once he was fully on top of the machine, she nearly fell backward.

"Inas."

"Yes?" he managed. She could see him beginning to sit up.

"There is a vent on the left wall of this place. Can you see it?"

Inas gazed at the left wall. His eyes slowly ventured higher and higher until the vent opening was in his field of vision. "I can see it. Is it large enough for a human to crawl through?"

"It looks like it is."

"Do you think we can climb to it?"

"It's worth a try," she shrugged. They both stood. "Also," she began, "don't look down."

Inas nodded, and they both began to move slowly across the elevator's surface. Once they had reached the edge of its left side, Dalia examined the wall ahead. The wall was a few feet from the elevator. *Don't look down, Dalia.* There were a few electric boxes here and there, as well as several firm, thin,

THE VOICELESS DREAM

horizontal metal, slinking around the walls. Dalia figured it was best to use them. But first, she needed to make the jump.

I need to grab something the second I jump, or else I'll fall to my death. I can either jump and grab the metal, while securing my feet, or I can fail spectacularly and leave Inas on his own. Dalia felt her legs tremble, and glanced at Inas beside her. He also seemed to be weighing his chances. *You're running out of time Dalia! Quit wasting it!* She gave God one prayer and threw herself over the edge.

When she had leapt, she felt no fear. Her eyes were only on the dirty metal bars in front of her. She suddenly felt the cold exterior of one beneath her feet. And she realized they had more width than she'd expected. Her hands had also managed to latch onto a long one, but its surface was slippery, and she could not hook her hands around any part of it. Her fingers ached as they held on.

Dalia looked back at Inas with large eyes. He gazed back at her with a hopeful expression. "Jump, Inas! But be careful. You have boots on and these bars aren't the ideal width."

"Ok. But if I die, I expect you to write on my grave: *It was Dalia's fault.*"

She rolled her eyes. Even in the most dangerous situations, he managed to say things like this. "And I'll make sure I'm the one who makes you fall if you don't hurry up." She began ascending toward the vent, placing her feet and hands on each winding cord and protruding steel piece she could feel. She had made it about ten feet high when she heard a *thud* beneath her. No. Below her. Dalia held her breath. *Either he fell and died, or he made it.*

The Voiceless Dream

She slowly averted her gaze below herself and saw Inas grasping the winding steel. She released her breath, and continued higher.

The climb was shorter than she had thought it would be and she was grateful for that. There had been too many close calls. Twice, she had heard Inas cry out when he lost his balance, but then would glance down and see him regaining control. She herself had lost count of how many instances she had misjudged her footing or when a cord had been too loose to support her weight. But they were here now. The vent was thankfully large. The very last thing she wanted to do was have to descend back to that jacked up piece of useless metal stuck in the middle of the shaft.

Dalia grabbed the edge of the vent once she had climbed high enough. She forced her arms to lift her body and crawled into it.

She sighed and gazed down the vent. It was dingier than the passage they had to climb through, and it smelled like dust and worn rock.

Dalia fell backward and stared up at the ceiling of the vent. She heard Inas clamber into it, his breathing audible. "I'm not cut out for this type of work," she said, her arms feeling numb.

"I can tell."

"Hey!"

"Usually, I would argue with you, but we don't have time."

The Voiceless Dream

"That's right," Dalia agreed. She looked at him, and saw his slumped form. But his face was not very visible. Inas's figure moved to a crawling position and then he pushed past her, trying to continue down the vent. Dalia was crushed against the side of the vent until he had finally moved past her, brushing her shins only.

"Why did you do that? I'm practically suffocated already as it is!" she shouted.

"You were taking too long to move, and if you hadn't noticed, we have some enemies trying to kill us," he answered, his voice a bit fainter than she expected. He was still making his way down the vent and was now much farther ahead.

Dalia re-strapped her gun onto her back and pivoted. The smooth metal pulled at the clothing on her legs, but she was able to finish her turn. Once she had managed the turn, she began to crawl, feeling her weapon scratch against the ceiling of the vent occasionally.

It seemed as if a long while had passed before Dalia spotted another opening in the vent. Light erupted from it and onto the top of the small metal tunnel they were crawling in. As expected, Inas reached it first.

"I found an opening!" he called back.

"I saw it too," Dalia asserted.

Dalia sat in front of the air vent's opening on the floor with Inas on the opposite side, facing her. She squinted down through it. The room it revealed was extremely bright, as if it

THE VOICELESS DREAM

had been painted from the light of the heavens. No one seemed to be in the room. Dalia fiddled with her long gun and moved it past her face. She angled it and slammed it against the air vent. The soft metal bent and after a few more attempts, it collapsed and plummeted to the floor of the room. Dalia cringed from the loud sound it had made.

"Go!" Inas ordered brusquely.

"You really like to state the obvious," she said in an irked manner.

Dalia released an agitated sigh and slipped her legs into the thin opening. Once her whole body was dangling in the room, she exerted more pressure on her arms and slowly lowered herself more until her head was in the room as well. She freed her hands from the metal that was cutting into them and allowed gravity to force her body downward.

She landed on her feet for an instant, but the impact was so strong that her knees gave way and caused her body to strike the hard floor. She rolled over, laying sprawled on the floor and looked up to find Inas looking down at her with an annoyed expression. She rolled over, moving away from her previous position, and watched as his feet made contact with the floor. He didn't fall.

Dalia stood and dusted herself off. By now, all she felt was perplexed and consumed. Her whole body felt so strained.

"We seem to be in a file room," Inas said, walking among the cabinets around them.

He was right. The room was large as well; it was at least five times as large as the cell. The black file cabinets were around the perimeter of the room and nearly touched the high ceiling. Dalia approached one in front of her. She tugged the drawer nearest to her open. Inside were several documents. Dalia lifted one from the organized row of the many documents. It was a packet. As she glazed her eyes over it, she saw that she was not able to comprehend it at all. It wasn't in her language. Only one paragraph near the top on the first page was.

"Inas, what is this?"

Inas walked over to her. He stood beside her and then snatched the packet from her hand. He examined it for a few seconds and to Dalia's surprise, he crumpled it and threw it across the room. It landed on the top of one of the file cabinets across the room. "It's an interrogation document," he said to her, gazing at where the crumpled packet had landed.

"How do you know?"

Inas averted his eyes to hers. His expression was dark. "I recognized it. When they interrogate us, they make us sign these documents or 'confessions' that are written primarily in their language. It's pretty cruel, if you ask me."

Dalia suddenly felt the temperature in her face increase. Her breathing became more shallow and rapid. She looked over at the open file drawer and seized a packet of documents from it. She ripped the pages apart, and let the wrinkled remains descend to the floor.

"What are you doing?" Inas shouted.

"I'm going to tear apart every single file in this drawer. Then we can leave."

"Dalia, this isn't a good idea!"

The Voiceless Dream

"I don't care anymore," Dalia told him in a loud voice. She continued to rip apart every piece of paper her hands held. "I bet you that none of these documents hold any true information. What kind of people are so immoral?" Her voice was rising. "What kind of people are this inhumane!" She tore the several wrinkled files left in her hand and then slammed her hands against the black drawer. It banged shut with a loud noise. Then, everything went still. Dalia stared at the file drawer with scorn.

"We need to leave," Inas said quietly.

Dalia began to move away from the cabinet. They walked off, located the door, and slipped out into the hallway.

The stairs were infinite. They must have been higher up in the building than he thought. He felt sweat trailing down his temple. They descended the steps, still running, and after one final turn, found themselves at their destination. The door to leave the dreaded staircase was only a few feet away.

Inas heaved out whatever heavy air remained in his lungs and slid down to the concrete floor. He settled on all fours and felt the icy floor meet his hands. He felt grateful for the cold that was spindling up his arms.

"Come on," Dalia urged, trudging past him. "I'm as tired as you are but we need to go! Who knows how much time has passed?"

Inas stood unsteadily, his vision dancing. He stared at the door in front of him and walked toward it. Dalia slipped past it when he had pushed it open and they made their way through a few short halls before finally arriving at the hallway of their cell. There were still no guards in front of the cell, nor in others around it.

Inas felt a rush of ease. He nearly forgot about his aching limbs. They began to make their way towards the cell door that now, had never looked more welcoming. They were only a few yards from reaching the deserted space.

"Halt!" someone called.

Dalia and Inas both glanced behind themselves. A man had his gun raised and aimed at them, only a couple feet away. Inas noticed Dalia moving to hide behind him. *She doesn't have her shoes,* he remembered. The man began moving in their direction, with a few of the puzzled guards glancing at the scene.

The guard was now only ten feet from them. He began to draw closer quickly. "Are you the runaway guards?"

Inas's chest tightened its knot the second he saw his face. He glanced past the troublesome man and saw that the other guards were attempting to not pay attention to them. "No."

"Yes you are."

"No we aren't." His head throbbed from the new anguish that was gnawing at it.

The armed guard was now only one step from them. His gaze was hard and accusing. Inas's mouth went dry. "I already said we aren't the runaway guards."

The man growled and pressed his weapon hard against Inas's chest. "You look familiar."

The weapon seemed like a rod that was trying to dig toward his ribs. The man exerted more force on it. Inas's legs

THE VOICELESS DREAM

felt as if they were about to give way from holding up his anxiety and pent up rage. Heat filled his face as he spoke. "You have no proof! Who are you to make such a claim?"

The man's hands began to shake. He lowered the weapon from its target, his eyes still challenging Inas's, and then stared down at the ground. "My mistake," he mumbled.

Inas huffed. "Leave," he ordered him. The man turned on his heel and walked back down the hall. They watched as he disappeared at the end of it, guided by its turn.

Dalia released a breath from behind him and was nearly gasping for air. She whispered with a fraught tone in her voice. "Go! Go!"

Inas shook his head vigorously, trying to get rid of the daze he had acquired from the cell guard. He could sense his heart clashing against his rib cage. He breathed in deeply, but his tangled emotions and thoughts did not loosen.

"I know that man," he whispered to Dalia, pivoting toward the deserted area. Dalia trailed after him and caught up with his long strides.

"What do you mean?" she asked.

Inas couldn't bring himself to answer her for several moments. "He . . ." Inas let that word stay suspended in the air. *I can't say it.* "He . . . was . . . one of the men . . . who killed my sister." He released the last words from his tongue like bullets. Quick and painful. His voice was quivering slightly.

Inas heard her breathing pause. "I'm sorry."

He stopped walking all of a sudden and Dalia turned to stand in front of him, so that her bare feet were less noticeable. "Why is he here though?" he asked himself.

THE VOICELESS DREAM

"He must have done something to lower his rank," Dalia answered, clasping and pulling at her fingers. He could tell she wanted to be in the refuge of the cell room rather than in the hall.

Inas rubbed his forehead and shut his eyes. He lowered his hand and advanced towards their destination.

When they finally neared the door, they both glanced to either side of themselves to make sure no one was watching them, and then quickly entered the cell. They took off the uniforms as quickly as they could, the possibility of death encompassing their heads. Dalia did not forget, however, to take the chain of keys out of her uniform. She stuck the keys inside her jean pocket, and then put the knife that had been holding the door open back into the leg pocket of the uniform.

They wrapped the clothes of the uniform around their weapons and helmets and set them out into the hallway as subtly as they could. Dalia shut the door silently. Both slipped on their shoes—left abandoned beside the door— in haste and ran back to where they had been sleeping, pretending to doze off. However, they kept their ears alert, listening for any sound, waiting as fear clutched their hearts. After many minutes, they heard a large number of heavy and loud footsteps approaching.

"Where did they go?" a faint voice asked, cutting through her thoughts.

The Voiceless Dream

"Maybe they were in a rush somewhere else," another voice answered. So the guards and the interrogator had finally arrived.

"But that doesn't explain why they would lie to me. I wasted so much time outside in the cold. Oh, and look! Your uniforms are over there on the ground," a third voice said. *That must be the interrogator. Oh no. I hope he isn't on to us,* Dalia thought.

"Why would our uniforms be over here? And how did we end up in a cleaning closet?" the first voice asked.

"Do you think someone from the cell did this to us?" a second voice suggested. Dalia felt her heart halt momentarily.

"Listen here, men. First of all, that cell door is impossible to unlock. It is stupid to think that a mere prisoner did this, especially with all of the guards that were here. They would have noticed something off about the two of you abandoning your shift. Right?" the interrogator asked the large group of guards.

"Yes, sir," they responded, almost in sync.

The interrogator continued, "We'll figure this out in the morning, or rather, tomorrow night. It's the middle of the night, and I don't have time for this. Everyone, get back to your posts." Dalia heard all the guards move about around the cell door. Within seconds, everything went silent.

Dalia sighed as relief swelled in her chest, and heard the guards scramble in front of the door. She was safe, for now. However, the interrogator did say he would figure something out in the morning. *Hopefully he won't think anyone in this cell did it.*

The Voiceless Dream

Dalia gazed up at the ceiling, laying on her back. All that her body wanted was sleep. But her head swirled unyieldingly with all of the events that had happened and the horrid feelings she had been forced to suppress. *I wonder what connection that man has to Inas's dead sister. How did she die? There is so much I don't know about her death. How did it cause Inas to end up here? What exactly did he do?*

Inas was laying on his sore back with his eyes shut. Every part of his body was aching and worn. He felt like a branch that had been snapped in half. He never knew it was possible to feel this horrible physically. But his mind was a different matter. *That killer. Why is he here? Why did I have to see him again?* Inas rolled onto his side, trying to fight the loathing feeling that was beginning to replace his misery. *Is it to remind me that I couldn't save her?*

Another Day, Another Plan

The next morning buzzed with liveliness as all of the prisoners in the cell talked and moved around. Even though she had barely been in their cell a day, they didn't give her much attention, and she was grateful for that. Dalia still felt exhausted and drained. But at least Abdul was happier now that she was in the cell with him, and he never left her side. He didn't smile, but luckily, he didn't scream either. Dalia ruffled his thick brown hair as he walked with her. She was walking over to grab a chair, when someone stepped in front of her.

The Voiceless Dream

"What is it, Inas?" she asked drowsily. He looked much more awake than she felt. It annoyed her.

"Remember we never got to finish discussing your whole escape?"

"Yes," she yawned, as she moved around him and grabbed a chair. She began carrying it back the way she came. Inas walked beside her.

"So do you want to discuss it now?" he asked.

"Won't the food come here soon?" she replied, as they reached the end of the room. She turned toward the far left corner, set the chair down, and sat on it.

"Fine," Inas responded. "We'll discuss it later." He walked away. Abdul sat down on the floor beside her chair. Only a few seconds had passed before Inas returned again, this time with a chair, and set it right beside hers.

She frowned at him. "Do you have no one else to talk to?"

"Who said I was going to talk to you?"

"You just did."

"Whatever," he replied flatly.

"How much longer will it be before the food cart gets here?" she wondered aloud.

"Why do you keep asking about that?"

She gave him an exasperated look.

It finally dawned on him. "You're scared they'll catch you. Well," he noted, "I think they should be here any minute."

"Then it looks like I'll have to hide," Dalia concluded. She glanced down at Abdul. He would definitely follow her and

The Voiceless Dream

give her hiding spot away. *I should have thought this through before. I could hide him with me, and make him believe it's a game.*

"So, how are you going to hide him when he follows you everywhere?" Inas asked her, looking at her brother.

"He's not the only one that follows me everywhere."

"Hey! I have my reasons! And you know them!" Inas retorted, offended.

Dalia rolled her eyes again, and then her tone became serious. "Do you think the man with the food cart will notice he's not present in the cell when he comes?" Dalia asked him.

"Probably. I'm guessing you're thinking of hiding your brother with you. How about tricking him to just stay with me insead?" he suggested.

"Maybe," she replied, with doubt fabricated in her tone. "But it'll be pretty hard to trick him into it. I'll just have to hide him with me."

"Do that then," Inas said evenly, not looking at her. "Hurry though."

"Ok, then. That's what I'll do," Dalia responded. She stood up from her chair, took her little brother's hand and walked over to his bed. She hid him underneath it first, and then slid beneath it herself. And just in time too. Only mere seconds had passed before Dalia heard the cell door slam open.

"Hurry! Hurry! I don't have all day!" the man grouchily ordered. Dalia clenched her hands. She glanced at Abdul and saw that he was covering his head with his hands. They remained concealed for only a few minutes longer.

"Psst."

The Voiceless Dream

Dalia swiveled her head to the source of the sound and saw Inas's tattered shoes beside her. "Can I come out now?"

"Yeah," he said.

Dalia rolled out, moving towards the other side of the bed and stood up. She pulled her brother out from beneath it and helped him stand. Together, they walked back toward Dalia's chair.

Inas was eating a loaf of bread. As she sat down on her chair he offered her some.

"Sure," she smiled, taking it from him. "Abdul." Abdul looked at the bread in her outstretched hand. He grabbed it and began chewing it slowly.

Dalia gazed at the prisoners in the dim cell . The one table with a few chairs was unoccupied for all of the men and boys were eating on their beds, together, talking quietly amongst each other. Some were eating rice, others bread. "Is all that they gave you?" she asked, astonished.

Inas shrugged dismissively and tore off a part of his loaf and answered her before eating it. "That's it. Yeah."

She sighed. Inas offered her more of his bread and she took it gladly.

"Back to the plan," Inas began. "Where should we start?"

Dalia finished eating her food and spoke in a quiet tone. "All we know so far is that I need to get to the equipment room sometime at night, put myself and my brother in cases, and get put on a truck and hope that it is heading toward our village to patrol that night. But, we never really figured out *how* I would need to get to the equipment room, or how I would keep Abdul's case from locking."

The Voiceless Dream

"Locking?" Inas looked confused when he heard the word.

"The cases I saw all had latches on them that locked when someone snapped them down. The only way I was able to keep mine open was with a hair tie. But, there were also other cases that had zippers," Dalia finished, as her memory began to aid her.

"Do you think he'd fit into them?" Inas wondered aloud.

Dalia and Inas looked down at Abdul, still sitting with his legs sprawled on the ground. He was seven years old, but he was quite slim and a bit short for his age.

"Well," Inas started, still analyzing Abdul by looking him up and down, "I think there are equipment cases with zippers that are large enough to fit him. Just choose the largest one."

Dalia tilted her head from side to side, considering his words. "I'll agree with that." She breathed deeply and glanced down at the floor. "Now, how will I *get* to the equipment room?"

Inas gazed up at the low ceiling of the cell. "This is tough," he exhaled, voicing her thoughts aloud. He looked back down at the stone floor beneath them and rested his elbows on his legs.

Dalia was also deep in thought. "You told me before that we can't use the food cart because we could get caught too easily, and we would not fit. But, last night we both made it out of the cell by dressing up as the guards."

"Dalia, that was a very dangerous plan, especially since we nearly got killed. I doubt those two guards will sleep on their shift again. Not to mention we might get caught by the other

The Voiceless Dream

guards beside our cell. We barely made it back. And what about the broken elevator?"

"Inas, we barely made it back because we had to get the keys and lie to an interrogator. I think the next time we try that idea again, it would be less risky. I mean, I have the keys, Abdul will be asleep, and the only thing I would really need to rush is finding the right case. Besides, if the elevator still isn't working by that time, just use the stairs and hide them someplace else."

"Ok, ok, fine. But how will you know when the guards are asleep?" he argued.

"I could just ask you."

"What do you mean?"

"I think we should wait until tomorrow night for you to check if they slept on their shift," she explained cautiously. She didn't want to rush him into her plan; she was still creating it as she spoke. It was best not to confuse him too much with false strategies.

"So, you want me to knock on the cell door in the middle of the night to check if they're asleep, and if they are asleep—which they probably won't be—then that night you'll leave with your brother by . . . ?"

"By dressing as one of them, and carrying him out of the cell. And if not that night, then the next"

"But where will you hide the guards? You can't leave them in the cell, because then they'll blame everything on everyone here," Inas remarked, outstretching his hand.

"Could you help with that?"

"Oh no. Do you mean . . . ?"

The Voiceless Dream

"Yes, I do mean *that*," Dalia replied, nodding.

Inas sighed and he put a hand on his forehead. He shook his head. "Fine, fine. So let's say this *actually* went as planned, tell me exactly how you will know that the truck you are thrown on will lead you back to your home? It was obvious to guess that as you were coming here, that it would lead back to this prison, but exactly how do you know that you will get back home on the truck you will be on if they all lead to the villages and towns around, and into, Gaza territory?"

Dalia took a deep breath and leaned against her seat. "This part of the plan, would be nearly impossible to solve," she started.

Inas nodded in a mocking manner, as his hand slid from his forehead to his cheek, with his elbow still resting on his knee.

Dalia tried to ignore him and continued. "When the truck stops at a village, I will hop out of it, and shelter myself and my brother there. I don't want to risk him waking up and making noise."

"Ok, but you still haven't exactly explained how you will get back home."

"That part is a bit more complicated."

"Care to explain?"

"No, not really."

"And why not?" he inquired.

"It involves lots of risks and luck that the right people will be there at the right time," she said as she reconsidered her idea. *It's not like every great plan has absolutely no risks at all. As long as I end up home, it'll be fine.*

The Voiceless Dream

Inas eyed her in an incredulous manner. "Ok, but where will you put the guard's uniform? You can't just hide it in the equipment room; someone would easily become suspicious."

"When you're done with your part, you can come down to the equipment room and bring the uniform back up. Just try to keep it well hidden from the other guards at the cell doors."

"Ok, and then I'd bring the guards back down, and then undress out of their uniform, and put them back on post."

"Exactly," she nodded.

Inas removed his arms from his thigh and sat up. "This isn't the best idea, but it isn't the worst either."

Dalia's head perked up. "So you're agreeing to it?"

"I suppose," he responded reluctantly.

"Thank you. I really don't know what else to say. I really can't thank you enough." She smiled as she felt relief flood over her. She turned her head away and glanced at Abdul. *I didn't actually think he'd really agree to it. Thank God he did. Now I can get back home.* She sighed again, but immediately felt an anxious feeling replace her relief. *But Dalia,* a small voice crooned in her head. *Don't think you'll make it out so easily. Something will happen.* At that instant, Dalia felt a foreboding feeling tugging at her heart. *Something's wrong. Something will happen.*

"Hey, Ran! Wait for me!" Matt called, as he ran down the hallway toward Ran, who was walking towards the elevator.

THE VOICELESS DREAM

Ran halted. Matt ran up beside him. "Remember that tonight we're going to the patrolling grounds, right after our shift is done."

"I hope I'll be able to make it," Matt told him. "Also, we need to take the stairs up. The elevator is broken and won't be fixed until tomorrow."

Ran groaned. "Let's go to the stairs then." They began walking back the way they came. "Anyway, why do you say that you *hope* you'll make it?" Ran asked him, irritably.

"Because I still haven't finished that *thing* I wanted to get done."

"And why couldn't you get it done?"

"I didn't have enough time. I hope I will tonight, after this shift."

"But Matt, we only have enough time to get up to the trucks before they leave, and besides, the General expects us there! We're his best soldiers!"

"So you're saying . . . " Matt trailed off, waiting for Ran to finish the sentence.

"I'm saying you can't finish whatever *thing* you need to do tonight, because we need to be at the vehicle lot by 9:30 sharp!"

"What about tomorrow night?" Matt asked.

"Sorry. Tomorrow as well. And the day after too. But don't worry," Ran said, as he patted his back roughly, practically slapping him. "The day after *that* we will have off."

"Do you think we'll have more time to get to the vehicle lot tomorrow, or not?"

The Voiceless Dream

Ran shrugged, and adjusted the gun on his back as he began jogging down the hall. "No. We have to be there again at that same time. We are only given five minutes to make it there."

"What about the next day?"

Ran considered the question, and then shook his head from side to side, still musing over the inquiry. "Possibly. If the next guards come early for their shift."

"Then I'm going to try and finish it before then."

"Why can't you just do it the day after?"

"I just want to get this task out of the way as soon as possible. Besides, it won't take long."

"I still don't understand why you wanted to guard those cells. We could have lost our positions if the General found out."

Matt shrugged.

Ran sighed. "Talking to you is like talking to my mother. You will never listen to me."

Matt laughed hostiley. "I know."

They had arrived at the door of the staircase. Ran opened it for them, and then they both began to descend it, their footsteps echoing against the stone walls surrounding the stairwell.

Tensions Rise

That day passed by quickly, and so did the light of the next, and soon, before Dalia knew it, the sun was almost gone. The other detainees there were all very polite to her and gave her some space. Once in a while, she and Inas would talk to them and she had found out that all of them wanted to help her escape.

Dalia knew she couldn't tell them her ideas for her and her brother's escape; she was afraid they would deem it too risky or dangerous to help. She had decided only to ask certain questions, ones that wouldn't give away too much away. At the small table in the far upper right corner of the room, both she and Inas now sat with two other prisoners.

Dalia asked them her questions carefully. "Do you know which villages the IDF trucks head to?"

The Voiceless Dream

Both of the men glanced at each other. A middle aged man, with a dark beard and thick build, named Ajas spoke. "Well, we don't know for sure. However, we do know that the trucks that leave the earliest head to the farthest villages first, and then one by one each vehicle goes to patrol."

The second man, named Hamza, interjected. "But they don't patrol everyday. They only leave on certain days."

"Which days?" Inas asked.

"It sometimes depends, but as far as I know they may be patrolling for the next three or four days."

"Do you know what time?" he asked again keenly.

Hamza put a hand on his bald head. "I'm pretty sure it's a number of minutes after the daytime guards get off their shift."

That's good, Dalia thought. *This should give me enough time to leave, and it should be enough time for those guards to maybe, just maybe, fall asleep one more time on their shift.*

"Thank you," Dalia smiled, and Inas echoed the words after her. They slowly rose and left the table, making their way to Abdul's bed. Abdul had fallen asleep only an hour earlier, and now as Dalia looked at him, she saw his cut was beginning to heal a bit but his bruises were still prominent.

She slid down to the floor and let out a deep breath slowly. She couldn't wait to go home and see her grandfather, but she felt fear at the idea of facing him again. Her job had been to protect her brother but looking at where they were now, she knew she had failed. Could she ever trust herself again?

The Voiceless Dream

"Dalia," Inas said, cutting through her thoughts.

"Yes?"

"Are we going to check on the guards tonight?"

"Yes. We'll pretend to go to bed like everyone else, and then once they're all asleep, we'll wake up and check on the guards."

"Ok. But, I'll warn you, I'm tired today." As soon as the last words escaped his mouth, he suddenly yawned and put a hand over his mouth.

At last, night had blanketed over the day, the light seeped away like flowing honey, and soon everyone was asleep. Everyone in the cell was asleep except for Dalia and Inas, however. Luckily, despite Inas's weariness, he stayed awake.

"Ok, how much longer till you'll check?" she asked him in a restless whisper, as they sat together beside her brother's bed.

"I won't check just yet. We need to wait a bit longer."

"But everyone else fell asleep a long time ago!"

Inas shook his head at her. "More like three hours ago."

She groaned, and swallowed, or rather, she tried to swallow. Dalia put her hand gently to her throat. *How long has it been since I drank anything?* She lowered her hand back down again.

Inas turned to her. "I think I'll go now," he whispered, and then stood steadily. Dalia watched as he made his way over to the cell door cautiously. Once there, he pressed his ear to the door and listened. Dalia waited with anxious anticipation for

THE VOICELESS DREAM

several seconds. Finally, Inas moved his head from the door, and made his way back.

"Why did you come back? Did you hear them?" she whispered as he sat down.

"Yes. I could hear them faintly talking. It's a good thing I didn't knock first."

"Do you think we should wait a bit longer?"

Inas shrugged. "What do you want to do?"

Dalia averted her gaze to the ground. *I want to wait longer but I'm scared it won't do any good, and we would have ended up wasting time. I'll just have to try again tomorrow.*

Inas cocked his head to the side. "Did you decide yet?"

"Yes, I did," she whispered warily. "Let's both go back to sleep. We'll see if they're resting tomorrow."

"Good idea." And with that last statement, he got up and walked back to his bed. Dalia laid back down and sighed. *I hope I have better luck tomorrow.* She was about to close her eyes when she felt something bump her. Startled, she moved away in fright, and looked down at the floor to find a thin blanket. She looked up and saw Inas standing in front of her, silhouetted by the orange light.

"You'll need that," he said, and walked away.

Dalia shook her head grudgingly at him as he left and snatched the white blanket. She draped it over herself and laid her head on her hands, beginning to feel grateful he had given it to her.

The Voiceless Dream

The next morning passed by in a blur. Abdul had been acting more agitated that morning, and it worried Dalia. She knew that the more agitated he got, the more likely he was to throw a tantrum. All she could do was hope he didn't. She was sitting on the cool concrete floor, with him right beside her, as the dingy atmosphere of the cell surrounded them. It had been a while since Dalia had seen pure sunlight, and she silently wished for it now.

Inas wasn't with them this time. He had left the cell escorted by guards, which were not—she had been told— the ones guarding the cell door. They had been of higher authority. Dalia had expected this to happen sooner or later. She only hoped he was okay. All that she was focused on now was keeping her brother calm. She glanced at him. *Just hold on, Abdul,* she thought. *Please don't yell or scream. Don't do that.*

But sadly, the world was against her wishes. Her brother screamed and sobbed only minutes after she thought this. Dalia tried to console him, but ended up hiding after she began to hear guards running outside the cell toward them. When they entered the room, their presence had caused her brother to become even more agitated.

They approached his bed and pulled him off of his bed. Dalia watched as their boots moved around it, and soon saw Abdul's small shoes join theirs. She shut her ears to his heart-wrenching screams as they dragged him out of the cell. As she heard the door close shut, she forced herself to roll out from underneath the bed, keeping her head tucked. She shook her hair out of her face impatiently, and stood up, with her heart beating fast.

THE VOICELESS DREAM

"Where did they take him?" she asked the men in the cell, looking at them.

They all looked at each other slowly, with worried glances, then looked back at her. "I don't think you'd want to know," replied one man timidly.

Dalia turned her face away from them, to keep them from seeing her fear and her watery eyes. *I will not cry. I will not cry!* She dropped to the ground in angst, and brought her knees to her chin. She kept her head down as she forced her tears back, and bit her lip to stop it from quivering.

Crying wouldn't help anything about this situation, and Dalia was beginning to feel that nothing, and no one, would ever really help her anymore. *But Inas helped you,* she thought to herself. *You are not fully on your own. The more you think this deprecatingly, the more you will act without thought.* Dalia breathed deeply. That was true. The more she lost hope, the more she fell into more trouble. She needed to keep her head up.

Dalia did not know how long she had been sitting beside Abdul's bed before she heard the guards fumbling with the door's lock. Her head jolted up, and she immediately rolled underneath his bed once again. She watched as light from the hallway seeped into the room as the cell door opened. She heard the men push someone into the cell, then slam the door shut. Dalia climbed out from underneath the bed and stood up. She walked to the other side of the room, hoping

THE VOICELESS DREAM

they had finally brought her brother back, only to find Inas in front of the cell door.

Everyone was crowded around him with concern. "Are you okay Inas?" Hamza asked, as Inas slowly stood and began dusting himself.

Dalia stood apart from the group examining him. He had two new bruises on his right arm, a long cut on the other, and he looked extremely weary and fatigued. Dalia wanted to know where they had taken him before, but was too worried about her brother to care now. She turned on her heel and quietly walked back to her brother's bed. She slowly lowered herself onto the stone floor beside it, and sighed with anxiousness, then rubbed her forehead in frustration.

"Dalia."

Dalia raised her head to the voice. *Inas. Of course it's Inas.* He seated himself right beside her. She lowered her head back onto her knees, and wrapped her arms around her legs.

Instantly Inas's expression changed once he caught a glimpse of her sorrowful face before she had hid it. "What's wrong?" When Dalia didn't answer he absently began looking around the room, and then it hit him like a train. "Where is your brother?" he asked, still looking around the room frantically for him.

"They took him," she replied, her voice wavering slightly as she raised her head.

"Why?" Inas asked, dumbfounded.

She still didn't look at him. She kept her gaze on the ground. "He had been agitated all morning but I didn't have anything to calm him down," she sighed.

The Voiceless Dream

"I don't think they'll do much to him."

"What do you think they'll do?" she questioned, staring directly at him. Inas averted his gaze toward the floor in front of him. She waited several moments for him to answer, but when it was evident he wouldn't, she decided to change the topic. "Where were you?"

He paused a second before he answered. "They took me back to interrogate me more. I thought they were done, but I guess I was wrong."

"What did they ask you? And . . . did they hurt you badly?" she added, as her eyes strayed to his injured arms.

"They didn't hurt me much. And they asked me questions about my sister and if I had any other living family members."

"I'm guessing they didn't get anything out of you?" she said solemnly.

"No, everyone's all gone."

Dalia grimaced. She wished she had the right words to console him, but what are you supposed to say to someone who had lost everything? Her words would sound hollow. "Do you at least have a little hope left for your life?" she asked quietly.

He didn't answer immediately, but then steadily responded, "Yes."

Dalia lowered her head back onto her knees. Suddenly, they both heard yelling and heavy footsteps outside of the door. Dalia's head shot up.

"Hide Dalia!" Inas yelled. Dalia didn't need another warning. She crawled below Abdul's bed and laid on her

The Voiceless Dream

stomach, waiting with anticipation and fear as she heard men enter the cell. The light from the hallway fell into the dim room, and with it were the heavy footsteps the men brought along. Dalia could feel that the whole cell was tense but she heard nothing, except the men entering the cell.

The men holding her brother dropped him to the ground and walked back out, their heavy boots making deep echoes. As soon as the door closed, Dalia climbed out and stood up. She looked ahead of her, and saw Hamza, Ajas, and another man helping Abdul stand on his feet. She paced over to him and walked him to his bed. He looked dizzy. Just as they approached his bed, he collapsed on to it, unmoving.

"Abdul!" Dalia panicked. She shook him, and turned him onto his back, and saw that his eyes were barely open. She put her hands on either side of his face, feeling tears sting her eyes.

Hamza's voice answered behind her. "I didn't want to tell you this, but I suspected it. Dalia," he began hesitantly, as his voice became stern. "I believe they shocked your brother."

Dalia almost fell to the floor. Her knees nearly buckled and gave way. She regained her posture and only managed to breathe out one response, with horror and shock flooding over her, as she gripped onto the reality of the word Hamza had uttered. "What do you mean they shocked him?"

Ajas's voice flew to her ears from her left. "Other than beating the children they detain during interrogations, the soldiers also are rumored to give them electric shocks."

Dalia could barely wrap her mind around what he just said. She fell to her knees and put a hand on her forehead, as

The Voiceless Dream

she felt her tears forcing their way past her dark eyes. Dalia buried her face in her hands and heard the prisoners behind her move about, leaving her be. She felt grateful that they gave her space. Only Inas had stayed and sat beside Abdul's bed with her. *Maybe this is all a nightmare.*

The Last Night

As the day finally passed a few hours later, the night came in, draining all of the light from the sky into its darkness. Dalia and Inas had stayed awake, still sitting up with their backs against the wall behind them, beside Abdul's bed. Dalia from time to time would place her hand on Abdul's chest to make sure he was still breathing. She had covered him with both his and her blankets as he slept, even if it wasn't much help from the frigid inside of the dark, grim cell.

"Can you believe you've been here for five days?" Inas whispered to her.

Dalia drew in a quick breath. *Five days? How did I forget so quickly? Why is time passing by so fast?* She released a heavy breath she hadn't realized she had been holding. Her hair fell into her face, and she brushed it back absently. She pivoted her head towards Inas slowly. "What time do you think it is?"

"I can't be sure, but I think it should be around maybe 9:00 p.m. by now," he answered, not looking at her.

Dalia glanced at Abdul, then gazed ahead. "How bad did they shock my brother?" she asked.

Inas was startled by the question. He tensed and then calmly whispered, "Are you sure you want to know?"

Dalia pursed her lips, then said, "Why would you answer a question with a question?"

"Because if you really want to know the truth, I have to make sure you are prepared to stay sane."

"Nevermind then." Dalia lowered her gaze back down to the ground, where her legs were stretched in front of her. She looked up at the ceiling. "Inas?"

"Yes?"

"Do you think the guards are asleep now?"

"Let's wait a bit longer before we check. I'm pretty sure that they've only been on post for maybe ten minutes.

"Ok, fine."

"Dalia?"

"What?"

"Don't feel bad about not being careful all the time."

Dalia suddenly whipped her head around and gazed at him in the darkness. "Why?"

"If you hadn't risked anything, you wouldn't have gotten this far. And you wouldn't have been able to see your brother for a long time."

The Voiceless Dream

Dalia stared at the floor and thought about his words. *In a way he is right. But that still doesn't help the fact that I may not make it out of here. Sure, risking something does gain you other objectives. But, it also gains you unwanted trouble.*

"I think we should go inspect them again," Inas whispered as he stood up. He tiptoed over to the door, and Dalia sat up straighter against the wall. She watched as Inas set his ear to the door and listened. After a few moments he pulled his head from the door, and set it back, listening harder for any sound he could hear. Then, slowly he lifted his head, and turned toward Dalia. He gestured in a frantic manner.

Dalia, bewildered and anxious, stood up as quickly as she could and cautiously moved to the cell door. "Are they asleep? Did you hear anything?" she asked softly, gazing at his apprehensive eyes.

"I didn't hear anyone out there. But to make sure, we need to knock."

"Knock then," Dalia replied breathlessly. She could be so close to finally leaving this prison and getting back home. Inas knocked on the door twice. Not one sound was made. Inas looked at Dalia wide-eyed.

Dalia moved past him, towards the long gap in between the door and wall, and pulled out her hair clip.

Matt walked the halls swiftly. He knew that the General was doing him a big favor by rearranging the guarding shifts. He had not been happy to find out that one of his best soldiers had "wasted time", as he put it, guarding. Matt had pushed his

The Voiceless Dream

luck to the brink asking the General if he could stall the patrol for twenty minutes. He had said he would consider it.

Glancing at his watch, he saw that his time was down to only 17 minutes. He increased his pace until he was at a run, and approached the elevator. He stepped inside and restlessly commanded it. Once the doors slid shut, he paced back and forth inside of it until he heard the *ding* of the elevator, and the doors opened again.

Matt dashed out towards the right, down the hall. His heart raced as he ran. He knew he only had a short amount of time to find what he was looking for. Soon, he neared the file and equipment rooms, their doors lined on either side of him. He fumbled with his keys and opened the first file room. *I just need to find that document. It has to be here.* He switched on the light, and immediately the room brightened. He ran over to the first file cabinet and pulled out the drawer. Frantically, he began searching.

Dalia and Inas had been able to easily pull the guards into the cell room. The other guards in front of the cells around them had been either distracted, tired, or had even given in to sleep. Once Inas had knocked them out and they had dragged them in, they kept the door open with one of Inas's shoes, and dressed into the soldiers' uniforms on top of their own clothes. This time, the men had new white shirts beneath their uniforms.

Dalia made sure she had cut their shirts up with the knife. She had also made sure to pull the keys from her pockets and

The Voiceless Dream

set them inside the uniform, and had hid her shoes in two large, separate pockets of the uniform as well.

"Ready?" Dalia asked, once they were done.

"Ready," Inas confirmed. Dalia nodded, and then turned on her heel, walking as quietly as she could towards her brother. Once she had neared his bed, she quickly scooped up his small frame into her arms, and walked back to the grim metal door.

"Let's go," she breathed, and Inas leaned down and picked up the two unconscious guards off of the ground. He slung one of each of their arms on his shoulders.

"They're a bit heavy, but I think I can manage," he replied with a somewhat strained voice.

"If you say so," Dalia responded, slightly concerned. "You leave first. I think it would be rather suspicious if we left at the same time."

"Good idea," Inas huffed, turning toward the door. Dalia opened it for him, using her other hand to hold her brother.

"And Inas," Dalia began.

"Yes?" he asked, looking back at her.

"Thank you."

Inas smiled at her. "You're welcome, Dalia. Good luck," he said, and then walked out into the hallway, his breathing loud.

Dalia watched him leave and began to impatiently await her chance to exit the cell. *I'm almost there. I'm almost there. I'm almost there.*

The Voiceless Dream

Matt had looked through several file cabinets already. He knew his time was running out. Soon, the soldiers would come down and begin loading the equipment cases, and weapons into the trucks. He began searching through the next file cabinet. Luckily for him, this one was smaller than the others.

He pulled open the first drawer. Nothing. Second drawer. Nothing. Third drawer. Nothing. Now he was onto the last drawer. He tugged the last drawer open and his hands flew between the documents. Finally, something caught his eye. It was the girl's picture. Matt breathed in astonishment as he pulled it out slowly. Yes, it was the girl. He looked at the information on her document. The first thing listed there was her name. *Dalia Dawashe.* Matt breathed in awe as her name rang through his head. *Dalia Dawashe. Dalia Dawashe. Dawashe. Dawashe. Dawashe.* It was her.

Dalia rushed down the hall with her head down, Abdul in her shaking arms. She was closer than ever to the weapon room now. And within seconds she reached it. She stopped in front of the door with anxiety filling her head and heart. Her head began to throb. By now, Inas must have nearly finished his part of the plan. She knew she would never be able to thank him enough for how much he had helped her.

She pulled the keys out of the pocket on her right thigh, and quickly searched for the one she had marked. She found it easily and she stuck it into the keyhole of the equipment room. It opened and she quickly stepped inside and shut the

THE VOICELESS DREAM

door behind her. She paused. For a second she could have sworn she saw someone else leaving the room in front of her, just as she had shut the door.

Dalia tucked the keys back inside the pocket and faced the room she was in, examining it. The room was dark and she could barely see anything. She was tired from racing so fast in the heavy uniform and from carrying Abdul. She breathed heavily and leaned her hand against the wall beside her to support herself, sliding it up. But, as she slid it up, she hit the light switch, and abruptly light flooded the room. Dalia jumped slightly, startled. She immediately shook her head in frustration. *Focus Dalia. Focus. Find the cases now.*

Dalia walked among the equipment, now organized in rows, and searched for a case large enough for her first, just like the one she had hid in a couple days ago. She easily found a stack of them at the other end of the room. Dalia pulled one of the metal cases off of the stack, and set it on the floor slowly. She reordered the stack of cases a bit so no one would be too suspicious. Then she desperately searched for a case large enough for her brother. The time was running out.

Dalia paced back toward the door, looking at each case, and then she turned behind them, and found another set, with zippers. Dalia let out a quick sigh of relief and pulled one off the stack, set it at her feet, and rearranged the cases as quickly as she could with her free hand. Her left arm ached from carrying her brother, but she couldn't rest just yet.

She lifted the case at her feet and ran over to the other end of the room, then proceeded to lift the equipment case she had picked for herself earlier. Dalia set Abdul onto the

The Voiceless Dream

ground lightly and slowly. Then she unzipped his case, unlatched hers, and pulled the weapons out from each of them. She carried each of the weapons and hid them behind the file cabinets on the far left corner of the room.

Then, she took off the guard's uniform that she was wearing and threw it, helmet and all, behind the cabinet as well. Dalia slipped on her white shoes, feeling extremely rushed. She ran back over towards Abdul and the cases, and pushed them over beside the other rows of equipment. She quickly fit him into his, and zipped it up, but not all the way so that he would be able to breathe a bit.

Dalia inhaled abruptly and then pulled out the hair tie from her hair, right behind her head. Her last hair tie. Her hair tumbled over her shoulders and stopped falling when it had reached its full length at her chest. Dalia snapped her hair tie and felt a brief stinging pain on her forefinger. The tie had turned into a stretchy band. Dalia tied the band onto the hook of the lock of her case, and knotted it three times.

Panic-stricken, with adrenaline coursing through her veins, and her heart beating in her ears, she squeezed herself into the weapon case, pulled the band inside with her, and shut the case closed. Almost instantly afterwards, she began to hear heavy and dragged footsteps outside the door.

After a minute of running with all of his might, Matt had finally approached the elevator. He gripped the document inside his palm tighter, wrinkling it, and stepped inside of it. He still couldn't shake off the feeling that there was someone

THE VOICELESS DREAM

inside the equipment room. He thought he had heard the door click. He shook his head. Right now, he needed to get back and get the General's truck ready for the night patrol. That had been the deal he had made with the General, or rather the punishment he had been given. As Matt exited the elevator, he saw a flood of soldiers coming down the hallway from his left.

He immediately recognized Ran among the group. "Ran!" he called. Ran gestured with a wave of his hand that he was coming, and jogged over to him.

"I thought the soldiers wouldn't be back yet," he said. *I still had maybe two to three minutes to get back to him before I had to load the trucks.*

"The General decided to let them grab the equipment, and he's letting the equipment trucks leave first. I mean, we are earlier than usual today," Ran explained, as other soldiers crowded around them, waiting for the elevator.

"He's not happy with me. He found out I've been guarding for the past—what?— five days," he said.

"At least you didn't smear my name. What did he punish you with?"

"Well, the only reason we're early is because I asked him to rearrange the guarding shifts and make them 15 minutes earlier. I asked him to stall the soldiers coming for equipment for twenty minutes. He said he would consider it, but it looks like he didn't fulfill it all the way. And he punished me by making me get his truck ready."

"Why did you want him to stall the soldiers coming in?" Ran asked.

The Voiceless Dream

"So that I would have enough time to find this," Matt replied, as he held up Dalia's document.

"Isn't that the girl?" Ran asked with his mouth agape, examining her picture. "I knew she had been detained before!"

"Yes, and you'll never guess what I discovered about her. She's—" But Matt was cut off as Noam came up being him and slapped him hard on the back.

"Hey, the General told me to tell you that *you* need to go check on that kid they shocked a few hours ago."

Matt threw his head back and sighed. He turned to Ran. "I'll tell you later what I found out," he said, shoving Dalia's interrogation document into his back pocket. Matt pushed past the soldiers crowded around the elevator and hopped in with the next group.

Inas had been able to carry the guards and hide them in the closet. He was more than overjoyed that the elevator was functioning. He sat on the floor now, resting for a minute. He hoped Dalia had made it to the weapon room fast enough. He had a lingering feeling that the patrol would be coming in for their equipment soon. *I should get the guards back before the soldiers get here. Who am I kidding? I have to.* Inas heaved a heavy sigh and stood up.

He opened the door and dragged the two unconscious men out and lifted them, with one of each of their arms slung around his shoulder. He trudged over to the elevator as fast as he could and pressed the lower command. It didn't open

THE VOICELESS DREAM

immediately. *Is someone there?* Inas thought as a sinking feeling entered him. *This isn't good. This isn't right at all.*

At that moment the elevator doors slid open, he quickly walked into the elevator. He set the men down gently and frantically pressed the elevator button. The doors slid shut and Inas's heart began beating faster. *I'm almost done with this. I just need to get them back, dress them, and pretend to sleep. Easy, right? Maybe I'm panicking for no reason.*

The elevator made a *ding* and the doors opened smoothly. Inas leaned down and hoisted the men back up. He pulled them out of the elevator and began walking down the hall, keeping his head tucked, glancing occasionally at the other guards at the doors.

Only a minute later, Inas heard the faint *ding* of the elevator behind him. His eyes widened and his throat closed. He looked behind him and saw that only a couple of meters away, a large group of soldiers were pouring out of the elevator. He swallowed and turned on his heel, trudging faster, until he finally reached the cell door.

He pushed it open and set the men onto the floor. *The patrol is here. The soldiers are here. But they weren't supposed to come back this early! How will I get that uniform back now? I can't just leave the guards out here!* he thought with panic. He glanced down at the guards at his feet.

"I'll just have to dress up one of them, and leave the other undressed, and then put both outside of the cell. Besides, all of the other men didn't even glance in my direction. I hope Dalia had enough time to hide that uniform well. I should be fine," he whispered to himself, trying to reassure his

THE VOICELESS DREAM

panicking head. *But will she be fine? Or has everything gone wrong?* He dismissed those thoughts.

Inas set to work, and soon he had both of the guards slumped against the cell door, with only one of them in uniform. He slipped on his shoes that had been keeping the door open and drew the other on. Then he cautiously shut the cell door and ran back to his bed blindly. He rolled onto his back and gazed up at the shadow-filled, low ceiling above him, and felt a foreboding feeling clutching his chest and tightening his head. *I hope you finished your part, Dalia, because I'm sorry that I wasn't able to finish mine.*

Run

Matt walked out of the elevator and turned left, moving farther down the hall. He needed to hurry to get the trucks ready for patrol, after checking on the boy. He grunted. The boy was more than a handful. Matt quickened his pace until he was at a run, but then almost toppled over as he stopped in front of the boy's cell. There, against the cell door, were two sleeping guards. But what surprised him more was the fact that only one had his uniform on.

"What the hell is going on here?" he whispered. Matt attempted to kick them awake. When they didn't move he tried again. No movement. They weren't sleeping, they were unconscious. He stooped to their level and checked their pulses and breathing, sighing when he knew they were still alive.

THE VOICELESS DREAM

Matt hauled them away from the door impatiently and dug into his upper right pocket, pulling out a set of keys. He quickly searched for the correct one, and then clicked it into the keyhole. The door opened slowly. Matt pushed it farther open and entered the dim cell, bringing light from the hall with him. He walked among the beds and saw that everyone within the cell seemed to be asleep. He made his way to the end of the room where the boy's bed was, but as he approached it, he saw no one there.

Matt's breath caught in his throat. *Where did he go?* He dropped to the ground and gazed beneath his bed. Nothing. He stood up and yelled, "Where is the boy? Where is he? Where is the boy!"

He watched as all of the prisoners awoke, some rubbing the sleep from their eyes. Once awake, they all gazed at him in unfiltered trepidation. Every single one of them stepped away from their beds and stood up.

"Where is he? Where is the boy!" Matt repeated sternly, glaring at all of them.

They all held faces of confusion, as they looked past him at Abdul's bed.

"We don't know," a small boy answered.

Matt shrieked with anger. He stormed out of the room, slamming the door shut behind him. Breathing heavily, he began to run down the hall, but ended up colliding into Ran within seconds.

"Ouch," Ran muttered, as he stood up rubbing his chest.

"The boy is gone!" Matt yelled, also regaining his posture.

THE VOICELESS DREAM

"What?"

"Yeah. The General is going to punish us badly for this!"

"But we weren't on post. The other guards were."

"Yes, but they were unconscious and one of them somehow didn't have a uniform on."

Ran's face changed from confusion, to realization, to a serious stare. He regarded Matt with a daunting voice. "I found a uniform in the weapon room just now, along with something else that you may want to see."

"What are you talking about?" Matt breathed with perplexity.

"Come with me," Ran said, and then they both tore down the hallway to the equipment room, as if the ground was crumbling beneath them.

Matt and Ran soon neared the equipment room, and they slowed their speeds to maneuver around the soldiers walking in and out of it. Once they had jostled past the other men, they entered the room with Ran leading the way.

"Look here," he panted, gesturing toward a file cabinet.

Matt inspected it. "There's nothing on it."

Ran gave him a weary look. "I mean behind it."

Matt moved around it, and there, concealed behind it, was a guard uniform and two guns. "How?" he breathed.

"I'm not sure. When I got here, I was pushed by some other soldiers, and I tripped, and there in front of me was this," Ran replied. "But one thing I'm sure of, is that we need to find that boy."

The Voiceless Dream

Matt clenched his fists in frustration. He glanced at Ran, and then sprinted out of the room, pushing other soldiers out of his way. Ran stared after him, with a baffled expression painted on his face.

"So Dalia left with her brother? How?" Hamza asked aloud. Everyone in the cell didn't utter a word. They all were either sitting on their beds, or standing up. Only one person stepped forward.

"Inas?" Ajas remarked, lifting his eyebrows. "You know something about this, don't you?"

"I helped her escape," Inas responded calmly. Everyone looked at him in awe, amid the dim light of the cell. He could see all of the ghastly expressions of the boys and men.

"That was quick. I was beginning to worry she would have to stay here for too long. She could have easily been discovered," Hamza commented.

Inas nodded. "It was easy for her. She's lucky to be small enough to fit in the cases."

"Cases? What are you talking about? What do you mean?" Hamza questioned, shaking his head in confusion.

Inas dropped onto his bed wearily and began explaining the escape that he and Dalia had created. Everyone gazed at him like he had gone insane. "However, I don't know exactly how she'll get back to her village," he finished. "She told me not to worry about it. And . . . there is one other thing I didn't tell you guys."

The Voiceless Dream

Hamza sighed. "And what might that be? That you were planning to try this yourself?"

Inas was taken aback. "No! Of course not! I didn't tell you guys about the part where I couldn't get the guard's uniform back." He paused for a few seconds. "Because the soldiers came to get their weapons earlier than we thought they would."

A horrified expression was settled onto every face in the cell, as they stared at Inas in disbelief. Inas felt a twinge of guilt grapple his stomach.

"What?" Ajas exclaimed in a whisper. "What if someone finds it, along with the guns Dalia had to hide?"

"I don't think they will. I know that she must have had enough time to hide them from the soldiers somewhere safe," Inas answered, drawing his words out cautiously. *At least, I believe she did.*

"Well, let's trust you're right. There's nothing we can do about this now. At least that boy can finally leave this place. Who knows how confused and scared he must have been?" Hamza said.

"Yes," Ajas agreed. "I'm glad they were both able to leave before too much trouble arose."

Inas looked away from them and instead rested his eyes at the floor below him where the lanterns radiated their small light. Fatigue began to cloud his thoughts and senses.

The journey up to the trucks hadn't been too bumpy, and Dalia's case swung less than last time. She didn't tremble

THE VOICELESS DREAM

much this time, because finally, weariness had caught up to her body and had taken over her mind. She just wanted to sleep, to fall away, but she knew that soon, she would need to unlatch her case so that she could breathe. Her stomach rumbled slightly. *Why am I always hungry at the worst possible times?* Dalia closed and opened her eyes slowly. *It doesn't matter. I'm going to get home. We're going to get home.*

Suddenly, Dalia felt a pain in her side as her case was thrown and landed atop the other cases with a hard thud. "Ouch," she whimpered, then cursed herself. She already had such little air to breathe, and now she was speaking. And then another thought slipped into her mind. *Wait. Am I going to be put in the bottom of this whole stack? How will I get out? Will it be too heavy? Oh no. I'll just have to push my way to the top to get any air.*

After several minutes, and several thuds above her, Dalia felt the vehicle engine hum and vibrate beneath her. Eventually, the truck began to move. Dalia tried to sigh, but realized she barely had any air left. *Oh no! I need to get out of here! And what if Abdul is running out of air or is being crushed right now?*

Dalia tugged the band in her hand, trying to open the case, and she heard a click. But the case's lid did not spring open. It stayed shut, only lifting up about a half inch. Dalia—who was laying on her side—pushed upward with her right arm, trying to open her case further.

She heard faint thuds and scrapes above and around her, as she pushed upward harder. Her arm began to ache but she urged it on, and soon, the case flew open, and her hand—that

THE VOICELESS DREAM

had been urging the case forward—went up with it. Dalia sat up from her tightly curled position, her legs bent in front of her, and took in large gasps of the cool night air. The truck was still moving, but she noticed that she had managed to move cases above her, not around her. There was still equipment obstructing her view in every other direction.

"I need to find Abdul first. I have to make sure he's okay." Dalia turned her body and head as she scanned the cases, hoping to recognize his. Not one around her had a zipper. Dalia began to panic and stood up, and there right in her field of vision were the many zippered cases. *I'll just look for the one that isn't fully zipped.* And with that thought in mind, she began searching.

She first examined the cases in front of her, and then when it was clear they weren't the correct ones, she hopped atop them and scanned the rest. She turned around and saw a moving zippered case. "Abdul!" she exclaimed, then immediately put a hand to her mouth. *Shut up Dalia. Someone could have heard you. It's dead silent.*

Dalia made her way around the hole she had created to open her case over to her brother's. She tried to unzip it, but the zipper was stuck. *Oh no!* Dalia pulled on it harder but it didn't budge. She felt fear rising within her, and then tugged as hard as she possibly could, with adrenaline coursing through her veins, and in an instant the case unzipped. She watched as her brother sat up, gasping for air.

"Abdul!" she whispered with relief. "I'm so glad you're safe." She embraced him. Abdul didn't hug her back, but he didn't resist her hug either. Dalia knew he didn't like to be

THE VOICELESS DREAM

touched or embraced, but she also knew he was scared, and she wanted to comfort her brother after everything that had happened to them.

He looked as if he would faint any second.

Dalia heaved a small sigh and began whispering more to herself than to him. "I know you don't understand me, and that you probably never will, but I just want you to know that I love you, and that I will always protect you. I know we will get back home. Just hold on. I'll get us home safe. Even if it's the last thing I do." She kissed the top of his head and looked up at the sky. One star was gazing back at her.

Familiar, a small voice rang in her head. Dalia felt her eyes widen. The voice continued with a sly tone. *Doesn't it remind you of the night you left for the patrolling grounds and that village man died? Of course, you thought no one would die that night, and even if anybody did, it would be yourself. But you were wrong. The man died.*

"Stop," Dalia breathed, holding her brother tighter, as fear hit her heart like a crashing wave. But the voice seemed involuntary. *Do you remember his family's screams the next morning? How the whole village had woken up to them? The man died. He died . . .* The voice left her head with a hiss. Dalia began breathing heavily, then looked around herself. *Did I imagine that voice? Was it a real person speaking?* she thought to herself, still shaken. But no one was behind her. Even Abdul was quiet. The only sound she heard was the faint hum of the engine. Nothing else.

The Final Phase

It seemed as if time had stopped as the vehicle sped down the endless road. Dalia and Abdul sat together quietly. Quiet was not something Abdul was much, but Dalia was relieved he was now, amid the dead silence of the night. Dalia could not see a lot in the dark, except for whatever the truck's headlights showed in the range of their white glow, which seemed to be only the dirt road.

Dalia huffed. *We've been on this road for so long. There has to be a village up ahead.* Dalia tilted her head back. She felt relief and dread at the same time, swirling in her chest, making her uneasy and tense. She wanted to go back home,

The Voiceless Dream

but she despised the thought of having to tell her grandfather where she and Abdul had been the last couple of days.

My grandfather for sure knows we're missing by now. Dalia slapped her forehead. *I should have thought of something else to say!* She heaved a small sigh. *There's no point in looking back now, Dalia. By morning, you should be at home.* She lowered her hand back down and clenched it.

After several more minutes, the equipment truck began to approach some sort of village or town. Dalia noticed this when she saw buildings in range of the vehicle's headlights. "We're here," she breathed. Dalia gripped Abdul's hand. However, as the vehicle crept closer and closer, she began to see that this was not a village. It was a town. The houses seemed a bit larger. It didn't have any destroyed homes and from what she could see now, she assumed she hadn't been here before.

Now all I need to do is find a way to get off of this truck. There are probably more behind it. It can't be the only one. And if it doesn't stop, how will I get off? Could I jump? Dalia clambered silently over the cases and looked down below the edge of the vehicle. *It's moving a bit faster than I'd hoped. If I did jump, I'd have to take the risk that I might break something falling, or Abdul might get hurt. Unless . . . there was something cushioning my fall. But what?*

She knit her brows in deep thought. "The cases are too hard," she began, then looked ahead. Luckily, they were still inside of the town or village or whatever it was. *Think fast*

THE VOICELESS DREAM

Dalia! She shook her head in frustration. *Maybe there might be something on the road, or beside a home to aid me here.*

She looked past the edge of the truck and then ahead of it, and mercifully, just a couple of meters ahead, was an object she could just make out. Then, in just a split second—as the truck moved closer, pouring its light onto it—it was what looked like a pile of torn white blankets with some wooden slabs on either side, in front of a small home, with one dim light glowing from the window.

Dalia wasted no time. She knew she could have overestimated the amount of blankets, and that there could only be one, but it was her best bet so far. The sooner she got off this moving vehicle the better. And in just the span of three seconds, Dalia had lifted her brother, paced over to the edge of the truck and jumped, making sure that once they fell that she could ease his fall.

She did end up making the fall a soft one for him, but not for her. She had been a bit too late, and instead of landing on the blankets—or rather, the blanket, as she saw it now—she had fallen feet first onto the three slabs of wood to the left of it. Two of them had collapsed onto her head, giving her a long cut from her temple and down her cheek, and now her feet ached and screamed whenever she moved them.

Dalia was still holding her brother tightly. Now she let him go, and he crawled off of her, and sat beside where she lay. She breathed heavily and tried to sit up, moving her feet out from under the wooden boards slowly. She put a hand softly to the cut on the left of her face and felt a stinging pain.

The Voiceless Dream

"Well, at least I didn't break any bones. And the truck is gone now," she added to herself as she leaned forward, looking down the road. The road ahead turned towards the right.

Dalia sighed and looked down at herself. She had dust all over her clothes and shoes. Her brother was still sitting quietly beside her. *Focus Dalia.* She snapped her attention back to herself, and attempted to stand up. Her shins and feet shrieked in agony as she stood. Dalia wanted to cry out, but didn't. She ignored the pain, and forced herself to stand.

Once she had accomplished that, she leaned her back against the freezing wall of the home behind her. *It hurts even when I'm standing up. If I try walking, or put any type of pressure on my feet, I'll drop. And I'm running out of time.* She searched around herself tiredly, and then her lazy gaze fell onto the blanket. *Perfect.*

Dalia slowly leaned down and grabbed the blanket. It wasn't too thick or thin. She attempted to tear it and succeeded. She tore it apart until she had two long strips of its fabric.

She glanced at her brother to make sure he was still there. Usually, he would be screaming with delight if he was in an unfamiliar place, but now, he seemed to be too frightened to do anything. He sat only a few feet from where Dalia was standing. Dalia turned her attention back to the fabric in her hands. She bent her knees a bit, and took off her shoes. She began to wrap the torn strips around her shins and feet.

"Done," she breathed when she had finished. She slipped her shoes back on, and began to walk slowly towards her

The Voiceless Dream

brother. This time, she only felt a slight sensation of pain. "Good," she whispered.

She lifted her brother into her arms and carried him. *I need to ask someone where I can get a wagon or vehicle of some sort.* Dalia looked at the home behind her. It was made of concrete, and was square in shape. *Maybe I could ask them.* Dalia walked around the pile of wooden boards and the torn blanket, limping slightly, toward the door. Dalia shivered as a cool breeze flew past them, and then she knocked on the door of the home.

She heard children's voices, and then a clatter, and then, finally, the door swung open, to reveal a woman, her hair covered with a scarf, wearing a long green dress that rippled with the slight wind at her feet. She had large blue-green eyes that looked tired now, and skin just like Dalia's. "Who are you?" she asked wide-eyed, looking both Dalia and Abdul up and down.

Dalia breathed heavily once, and then began to speak. "I'm so sorry to bother you at this time of the night, but I need to ask you a question." Dalia knew that she and her brother probably looked crazy, with dust all over their clothes, and cuts and bruises covering their skin.

The woman stared at them, and then smiled meekly. "Of course, but first please come in," she invited, gesturing towards her home.

Dalia looked past her inside her home. It had a strange glow that resembled the lanterns' in the cell. She began to tremble. "Oh, no, we really couldn't. We need to get home really soon, but thank you."

THE VOICELESS DREAM

The woman nodded her head. "I understand. But are you sure? It's cold out here. At least let me get you some food," she insisted.

Dalia was about to refuse the offer, but she realized her brother might be hungry. She looked back up at the woman. "Thank you. Do you have any tomatoes or bread?"

The woman looked at her with a concerned and bemused expression, but she nodded, and walked back into her home. Dalia sighed, and a few seconds later, the woman came back with a loaf of warm bread and a tomato.

"Thank you," Dalia smiled, taking the bread and tomato into her hand.

"Your welcome," she replied, "Now what is it you wanted to ask me?"

"I wanted to know if there is anyone here that can take me and my brother back home. I'm sure my village isn't too far from here."

The woman averted her gaze from Dalia and her brother, to the ground, in thought. Then she raised her head. "There is a man at the end of that road," she began, pointing to the right of herself, "But to reach him, you must make one left turn, and two right turns. He has a donkey with a small cart attached to it that he may let you ride."

Dalia raised her eyebrows. "May?"

The woman smiled a small smile. "You'll need to bargain with him. It may well depend on how long or far the trip is."

Dalia nodded at the woman. "Thanks again. Have a good night."

The Voiceless Dream

"Good luck," the woman replied, and with that, she shut her door softly, leaving Dalia and Abdul in the darkness of the night. *It's a good thing I saved those coins. Hopefully that will be enough to bargain with the man,* Dalia thought.

She looked down at her brother, then at the food in her right hand. "Let's feed you Abdul," she said, as she set him onto the dusty ground, Abdul slumped tiredly against the wall, his eyes drooping.

Dalia began to rip the bread partially through it's inside. Then, she compressed the tomato in her hand, and set it into the bread. She gave it to her brother, but he barely turned an eye toward the food. She pulled a chunk off from the loaf and fed her brother. He slowly ate it.

"Time to go," she said to him when he had finished. She lifted him into her arms again. *Now what was it the woman said? It was one left turn and two right turns down the road to . . . the right.* Dalia turned her head to the right, and then she heard something. It was very faint, and was a faraway sound but it kicked up her nerves. *Hurry,* a voice in her head hissed. *They are coming.* Dalia began to sprint down the road as fast as her injured legs and feet could carry her, with her heart beating in her ears. *Hurry. They are coming. They will kill you.*

Almost There

Dalia ran with all her might, while trying to put all the will she had into ignoring the pain spindling up her legs and all over her feet. *Keep running*, she thought to herself desperately. *Just keep going!* Dalia took the first right turn. Only one more to go and she would be at her destination.

Though it was dark, she relied on the brightly colored homes to help her identify her way through the winding streets. She knew her shoes were kicking up dust beneath her, but she was too panicked to care or slow down now. Even if her shoe prints were visible on the path, it wasn't as if the IDF was searching for any abnormal signs. Well, Dalia hoped they weren't. She kept her mind focused, and gained energy solely from her own fear.

The Voiceless Dream

Once she had made the last right bend, she ran on for only a few more minutes, and then stopped when she noticed a strange figure in the darkness. Dalia breathed heavily, panting. Her legs and feet screamed with agony, as she finally couldn't force herself any longer to ignore the pain. And she was so thirsty. Her throat felt as dry as the road beneath her. Dalia, still carrying her brother, limped towards the figure outlined in the darkness. *This has to be the man the woman was talking about. And if it isn't I can always run.*

As they approached the abnormally shaped figure, she began to feel her eyes adjust to the darkness, and there, sleeping atop of the cart, was a man. Just a few feet away from the cart, was a donkey also fast asleep. Relief flooded over her. She rushed over to the man on the cart.

"Excuse me, sir?" Dalia demanded, with anxiousness prevalent in her voice. When the man didn't move, she began to shake him awake, fear rising in her heart. *Wake up! Please wake up! They are coming for us!*

Dalia raised her voice to nearly a yell. "Wake up, please!" She removed her hand from his arm, and waited a few moments. Then jumped suddenly when she heard something moving behind her. She turned her head in alarm, and then was face to face with the donkey. It began to sniff her and her brother.

Once the donkey had stopped examining them, it looked back up at Dalia. It's eyes were nearly the exact color as hers, but unlike Dalia's eyes, the donkey's were harder to read.

THE VOICELESS DREAM

"I see you've met my donkey," a thin voice said behind them. Dalia stood petrified, then looked back at the cart. The man was awake.

"Y-yes, sir," Dalia stuttered. The man was dressed in a gray shirt and jeans. His face was thin, but his eyes were bright. He was an old man, but he slipped off of the cart with agility.

"Are you the voice I heard?" he asked her, standing with his arms crossed.

"Well, yes, if the voice in your head was telling you to wake up."

He smiled. "Why did you wake me up? The darkest hour of the night is upon us and I was dreaming a very good dream."

"Really?" Dalia asked, tilting her head to the side slightly.

The man sighed. "Why did you wake me up?" he asked again, with a more serious tone to his voice. "You know, it's strange. Of all the years I've been doing this, I've never seen two bloody, tired and desperate kids ask for my help. You look like you came out of a battle zone. What happened to you two?"

Dalia straightened herself, and looked him in the eye, feeling the donkey breathe down her neck heavily. "Listen sir. My brother and I need your help. We need to get back home before the morning. They are coming after us!" she whispered, pleadingly.

The man unfolded his arms. "Is it who I think you mean?"

Dalia nodded rapidly in response.

The Voiceless Dream

"Then get on the cart! Let's hurry now. And when you are settled tell me exactly what your village is called," he commanded as he ran over to the front of it.

Dalia obeyed, and then lifted her brother onto the cart. Then she hoisted herself up beside him. Her legs and feet immediately ceased their aching as she sat down. Her brother had fallen asleep.

She heard a *clunk* and pivoted her head slowly to her right to see the man attaching the donkey to the cart. Soon he himself hopped onto the front of the cart, and commanded the animal to proceed forward. He asked her the name of her village and Dalia answered him.

"Oh, well then it should take maybe around an hour to get there by donkey. Although, this donkey was woken up in the middle of the night, so it may take longer than usual."

'That is fine," Dalia yawned. "Just drop us off at the southern end. Here is your money," she added, pulling out the pouch from her pocket.

"No, no, no! You do not need to pay me."

"Are you sure?" Dalia asked, lowering her outstretched arm.

"Yes."

"Very well." She put the pouch back where it had been. "Do you know what time it is?"

"It seems to be two in the morning," he answered. "But, I could be a little off."

"Thank you," she replied gratefully. *I should get back home somewhere around three. I'm sure my grandfather should be asleep by then, and when he wakes up, he'll see us there with him. Maybe*

The Voiceless Dream

he'll just believe it was a nightmare; a figment of his imagination that we were ever gone. She turned her attention to the road behind them, and strained her eyesight. In the distance, at the other end of the village, she saw a light. A moving light. *I hope that is a figment of my imagination.*

Dalia forced herself to stay awake as her brother lay sleeping soundly on the cart. She would need to keep from dozing off if she was going to make her way back down into the village and stay clear of the IDF soldiers. Of course, the southern end of the village was always guarded last. She knew, after years of observation, that the soldiers would begin unloading soldiers in the northern end, then the west, east, and finally the southern end. Dalia assumed that the military command car she and her brother had been on was one of the first few that were deployed.

She glanced over at the man driving the cart. "What is your name?" she asked quietly.

"Ori. That is my name. What is yours?"

"Dalia."

"And your brother's?

"Abdul."

Ori nodded. "How did you two end up in that town?"

She sighed and put her head in her hands. "It's a long, long story."

He nodded again in response.

The cart sped over a few bumps and inclined a little.

The Voiceless Dream

"You two looked very beat up the first time I saw you. I hope you didn't run into too much trouble. At least you're alive."

"Yes," Dalia agreed, not looking at him. "Thank God for that." She rubbed her head as a headache began to persist at her temples.

The rest of the journey continued in silence.

Forlorn

The last living time of the hour trickled away as quickly as tree sap. The night was still as dark and cold as ever, and the only bright thing in the sky was one shimmering star. Dalia still remembered what that strange voice had echoed into her head. She shivered, and not from the cold atmosphere this time. *Don't worry about that Dalia,* she scolded herself in her head. *Focus! All that you need to do when the cart stops is run back into the village as fast as you can, and then back home. You are so, so close! Once you're home, then you can rest and relax. Focus.*

She put her arms in her lap, hoping she could run fast enough back into the village with her injuries, and if not, she figured she could just force herself to forget the pain. *I just want this to be over. Just let this night end.* Dalia had already begun to feel weariness flow over her, and there was little she

The Voiceless Dream

could do to stop it. The only things keeping her awake were her thoughts. She clung to them as if they were her last breath of life. All of a sudden, Dalia felt the cart lurch to a stop. She held Abdul steady as it halted. "Did we make it?" Dalia asked Ori.

He slipped off of the cart. "Yes. We've made it, but not fully all of the way. You can see your village in the distance over there," he explained, pointing ahead of them.

Dalia moved her gaze to where he was pointing, and strained her eyes through the darkness. In the distance, down the path, she could see small buildings jutting upward, with a little bit of light surrounding them. Her village.

"Well . . . we're a bit farther than I thought we'd be," Dalia stated, scanning her surroundings.

"I'm sorry, but this is the farthest I could go. I'm sure the patrols will be here soon. If I got you right up to the outskirts, then as I would be heading back I believe the patrols would show up. Their trucks are a lot faster than this donkey," he added, patting the animal, as it kept it's head down sniffing the ground.

Dalia shook her head in a casual manner. "I understand. I should be able to make it back from here." She looked back at her brother. *Should I wake him up? No.* Dalia slipped off of the cart slowly, putting one foot before the other. She then pulled her brother's small body off of the cart and lifted him into her arms.

"You should get going now," Ori said. "They'll be here soon. Goodbye, Dalia, and good luck." He patted his donkey

The Voiceless Dream

with one hand, and waved to her and her brother with the other.

"Thank you again," Dalia smiled. "Goodbye." With that last statement, she turned and began to race as fast as she could toward her village. Her heart was finally filled with hope, and she paid no heed to all of the pain she felt both physically and mentally.

Ori stod for a second, watching as the girl ran, carrying her brother. He turned his attention to his donkey. "You did good," he praised it, petting it's smooth gray hair. He climbed back up onto his cart, and directed his donkey to turn back the way they came. The cart pivoted around and then was pulled forward. The wind made a rushing sound. No. There was no wind tonight. Ori felt his heart beat speed up as his senses became more alert. He looked ahead and saw one moving light. A truck. That was the rushing sound. And it wasn't that far off.

Ori's voice emphasized a serious tone to his donkey. "Run. Go! Move left! They'll see us!" His donkey obeyed and began to pull the cart as hard as it could to the left, off of the path. The cart rattled faintly.

After a few moments, Ori looked back at the road, and saw the military truck pass over it in a fleeting second. Ori's eyes widened. "Dalia's in trouble. I can't do anything to help her now. I'd be too late." A sinking feeling began filling his heart. But not for himself.

THE VOICELESS DREAM

Dalia breathed audibly as she ran, but not from tiredness. She knew she was as close as ever to home now. So close to fixing this mess. And with every step she took, her hope increased. She tried not to move her arms much as she ran so that she did not shake her brother awake. She figured that the longer he slept, the faster the drugs would leave his system.

Her village became nearer and nearer. It seemed as if she could almost touch it. She was only fifty yards from the entrance of the village. Thirty from the outskirts. The cold air didn't cling to her skin as she ran, but nevertheless she heard a peculiar rushing sound behind her, as if the wind was moving as fast as her. *That probably is just the wind,* she thought to herself. But for some reason, she felt dread limbing up over her heart and all over her body. Nothing was right.

Dalia's heart leapt to her throat as she felt her eyes enlarge in the dark, and they stopped their focus on the village ahead. She began to veer off of the road, to her left, from shock and soon was completely off of the path. She couldn't focus. Someone, or something was behind her, but she didn't want to look.

Suddenly, Dalia's foot dipped off of the ground and into nothingness. Dalia cried out in fright, and immediately pulled it back up, falling to the ground. Abdul was still in her arms as she lay there, sprawled.

Dalia loosened one hand from her brother and slid it along the ground, towards the place where her foot had felt no solid ground beneath it. As she slid it, she soon felt the

The Voiceless Dream

dusty terrain disappear beneath her fingertips once again. Her eyes widened, and she approached it, crawling slowly toward it, with her outstretched hand guiding her. Dalia gazed below her outstretched hand. And there, right below her fingers, was a cliff's edge.

She sucked in her breath sharply, and gazed down at it. Though it was dark, she could tell it was a long fall. It looked like oblivion. Looking ahead she was able to make out lights in the distance. *I almost died. I almost killed my brother and myself.* She shook her head viciously in frustration. *Get back up Dalia! Get up! Focus! Focus!* She immediately stood, but as she did, the sly voice in her head came back. *Look behind you, Dalia,* it hissed, echoching all throughout her head. *Run.*

But before Dalia could even turn around, she felt a hand on her shoulder. Her heart almost halted entirely. Her body felt petrified, and even her legs and feet no longer seemed to radiate their pain. Dalia didn't even breathe as she turned her head slowly to look at the hand on her left shoulder.

And as she laid her eyes on the pale hand, she almost dropped to the ground in horror. Because there, on the back of the hand, was a long dark scar circulating back beneath it to the palm. And as Dalia moved her eyes farther up past the hand, she saw an even grislier sight. The face of the man was something she had feared seeing her whole life. From his eye to his cheek, ran another long dark scar.

And Then There Was One

Dalia stood breathing heavily, her arms shaking as she held her brother, with her head turned towards the soldier behind her. It just couldn't be. She could barely believe what had just happened. *It's him! It's him!* her head screamed. *He's right there!*

Dalia closed her eyes shut and opened them again. He was still standing there, his hand gripping her shoulder, and his mouth curved up into a dangerous smile. Dalia turned her head and body around and began to sprint. Fear ran all throughout her veins with excessive amounts of adrenaline, as every nerve in her body shrieked to run faster. She couldn't even feel the pain in her legs and feet any longer. She was too full of fright.

The Voiceless Dream

All of a sudden, a loud gunshot sounded throughout the night. Dalia cowered her head down and looked behind her. The man, her parents' killer, was holding a large gun in his hands, aimed right at her.

"Stop!" he yelled. "Put your hands up, and walk over here, or else I'll shoot you right where you are!"

Dalia gasped with fear and felt tears begin to leave her eyes, trailing down her cheeks slowly. She halted abruptly and turned around to face the man. *How did this all go so wrong, so quickly? How?*

Without putting her hands up, she began to walk slowly toward the man. *Think of something! Think of something! Dalia you are going to die!* But she knew there was no way out this time. If she ran, he would kill her and her brother. She didn't have enough time to think of any plan, and she knew the man wanted to kill them. *But does he know who I am?*

As Dalia stopped walking only a few paces from the man, she forced herself to quit crying. *Don't let him see your fear. Don't give him that satisfaction,* she thought to herself. *If anyone is going to die tonight, it will be yourself, Dalia. I will not let him kill anyone else.*

The man still had his gun aimed at her. His smile looked like a disease to Dalia. Then he spoke. "Dalia Dawashe. And I'm guessing that is your sleeping brother," he added, using his gun to point at Abdul.

Dalia felt her heart stop for a second. *He knows my name! He knows me!*

The Voiceless Dream

"You know, Dalia, you look so much like your mother. I raced here to find your brother, but, as an extra, I ended up finding you as well."

Dalia didn't breathe. She only kept her eyes focused on the man's. *Why isn't his voice raspy, like the one I heard in the equipment room? Isn't he the one who killed and slit marks on my parents?*

"I'll let you know that your brother was doing quite well in our facility. He was quieter, and more disciplined."

Dalia glared daggers at him. She wanted to hurl every curse word she knew at him, but that would easily get her to death's door. "How did you find me? How?" she asked, her voice coming out slightly uneven.

"It wasn't too hard. I'm sure you remember the last time you got detained," he began, as he pulled out her wrinkled document from his pocket.

Dalia's eyes widened with horror.

"And there on your document, your name is printed right at the top. Dawashe. You and your brother had looked so familiar to me from the start," he continued, putting the document back into his pocket. "And only a couple hours ago, I was told to check on your brother. When I went into his cell, he was not there, and only one of the guards had a uniform on. Luckily for me I have a very dependable friend. This friend was also the same man that slit your parents for me."

Dalia gave him a cold stare. *So there were two men involved in their death.*

THE VOICELESS DREAM

The man was still talking with a mischievous voice. "He came with me to the weapons room, and there we found the missing uniform and two guns."

Dalia felt baffled and distressed. *I thought Inas got rid of them... What happened?*

"Sadly for you, I had convinced my general to let the troops head out earlier today. Maybe if we had stalled longer, you could have bettered your little plan"

Dalia breathed out with muted shock. *Why were they early? Why?*

The man continued. "And along the way, I saw you, and with you was your brother. You were the one who helped him escape, weren't you Dalia?" he grinned, as he pointed his long gun at her.

"Listen," Dalia began boldly, surprising herself. "If you are going to kill anyone tonight, it will be me, not my brother. Torture me, hurt me, kill me! I won't care! But don't touch him!"

Matt was caught off guard by Dalia's lack of fear. He forced himself to maintain his expression. *Where'd your fright go?* He sighed. *Let's see if you'll keep this act up.*

"Unfortunately, I did come for your brother. I'm going to need him to come with me."

Dalia knitted her eyebrows. "You really think that I'm going to give him to you that willingly?"

"Who's the one with the gun? You or me?" he laughed.

THE VOICELESS DREAM

Dalia huffed out a deep breath. "Just kill me and leave him alive. We're the same flesh and blood anyway."

Matt grunted, and then smirked. "Your brother has a sentence to his name, which he has to pay. He needs to stay in that facility for three more months."

"I'll serve his sentence. I'll pay it back. Just leave him be," Dalia responded sharply.

"Listen little girl," Matt began impatiently, "I will kill both of you, if you don't stop talking. Give me your brother, and then walk back to whatever hole you came out of!"

Dalia gazed down at the ground in thought, with the man's gun still pointed at her and her brother. *Even if I was stupid enough to willingly hand him Abdul, he'd kill me afterwards anyway. It's obvious he wants to. But if I resist, maybe I can buy myself some time to figure something out. Maybe I could get his gun. But how? He could shoot in an instant, and I could get myself completely obliterated, and then he would take Abdul. I should just keep him talking.*

"I'm sorry, but . . ." Dalia said, feeling tears sting behind her eyes. "I do have a question though."

"What the hell is it?" the man demanded impatiently, with an exaggerated breath..

"What happens if I don't give my brother back?"

The man smiled. "Then I'll kill both of you without a second thought."

"Without a second thought?"

"Without a second thought."

THE VOICELESS DREAM

I want to know what his answer is to this question. "Why are you doing this?"

"Doing what?"

Dalia swallowed. "Why do you want to kill us so badly? What will it earn you?"

The man answered in a quieter voice. "You know why. My people waited centuries to return to this land after being persecuted elsewhere and now we finally are so close to regaining Israel's old territory. But you people didn't want us to build a state on this land."

"Because we were living on it, and have been for several centuries," Dalia answered. Her arms were trembling. "It's not our fault you were persecuted, and I don't know why the army and government are so against us."

"The only way to achieve what we want is to get you off of it. That is what I'm doing. What could your life have amounted to anyway? You're poor."

Dalia hesitated. His last sentence had stopped her for a moment. But she regained her hold on her thoughts and spoke with as much confidence as she could muster. "I know not all of your people think the same way as you. You're the insane one."

He revealed a small smile. "Tell that to my army. Tell that to the government. We're the ones with the force and power to drive you out. But why you've stayed like unmoving statues to your land and survived is beyond me. You'll see, though. You won't last much longer."

THE VOICELESS DREAM

Dalia glanced up at the sky, and then lowered her gaze back down towards the man. "How much longer until the other military vehicles get here?"

The man smirked. "You have no idea what is about to happen, do you? They'll be here any second."

Dalia swallowed, and then took two steps toward the man. "How much time exactly?" *Careful Dalia.*

The man squinted his eyes at her, his face a suspicious expression. "Maybe only three min—" He didn't get to finish his sentence, because right at that moment, Dalia tripped him with her foot and sent his feet sliding out from under him. His gun fell a few feet from his hand.

Dalia rushed to grab it, but so did the man. She couldn't throw herself at it, as the man was doing, because she had to hold her brother. He reached it first. *NO!* Dalia screamed inside her head as dread struck her. *That didn't just happen! No! No! NO!*

Matt gave her a devilish look, a look that said, *I'm about to kill you.* He stood up, holding his gun tightly. He aimed his gun down at her, then quickly lowered it towards her brother.

Dalia immediately noticed this, and turned herself, facing away from the man.

"Turn around!" he demanded.

"No!" Dalia shrieked back, tears flowing down her face. *I won't let you die Abdul.*

The man moved himself to face her, but Dalia only turned the opposite way again. Then, he suddenly grabbed her arm with one hand, attempting to make her drop her brother. Dalia held Abdul tightly with her other arm and

THE VOICELESS DREAM

hand, breathing heavily while facing him for a moment before she turned around. But a moment was enough for him, because in that instant, he shot at them, just before Dalia pivoted back around.

Dalia stopped moving, her body now turned away from the man. But nothing happened to her. She didn't drop to the ground and she felt no pain. That could only mean one thing. *No. No! No! No! Please let me be wrong!* It felt as all time had halted and disintegrated as she slowly lowered her head and looked down at her brother in her arms. Blood was splattered all over his shirt. And it was beginning to drip onto her hands.

"NO! NO!" she screamed as more tears began to trickle down her face. "NO! NO! NO! NO! ABDUL!" she cried as she fell to the ground. She lowered him onto the ground slowly, and looked at him with tears still falling from her horror-stricken expression. She couldn't speak or scream any longer. Only her soul was screaming, and it was screaming with agony. It was screaming as if a spear had plunged through it.

Dalia shook her hands around frantically. Her mouth moved, trying to form words, trying to form a voice, but not one sound came out of her mouth. Her tears dripped off of her face quickly. She threw her hands onto her head and shook her skull vigorously.

Now it's your turn, Dalia." The man made his way back around her, and faced her. Dalia couldn't even look up at him. She was still in too much shock to do anything. She

THE VOICELESS DREAM

shook her head as she continued to sob and clutched her shirt tightly in pain, beginning to choke on her tears.

The man raised his gun up, aiming it at her. Dalia braced herself, knowing she was about to die and join her brother to wherever his soul would be. She watched as Abdul's blood began to pool around him and soak her jeans. Her tears dripped onto his wound. *I'm coming, Abdul. I'll be with you again. I'm coming to join you.*

Trekking through the village everyday and looking in every sector was not easy, especially for someone as old as himself. Ever since the day he had realized they were missing, he had searched every day and every night hoping they'd show up. All that he wanted was his grandchildren back. He only hoped they were safe.

Now he was nearing the outskirts of the village. He limped as fast as he could past the last building, breathing heavily. He knew that in only a matter of time, the military trucks would arrive and file around the village here. He had to hurry. The old man began to move faster, as this thought stayed glued to his mind. Though it was dark, the bright homes helped him find his way.

Then, he heard a cry cut through the night. He lifted his head up and tried to look along the terrain. He couldn't see well at all, so this did not help him. Gradually he began moving as fast as he could toward the direction he had heard the pained cry. *Is it them?*

THE VOICELESS DREAM

After a few minutes he looked up again and scanned the terrain. And even with his bad eyesight he was still able to see the scene in front of him. He gasped as fear began to cloud him. There, only a few meters ahead, was a man, a girl, and a boy. But that wasn't what frightened him. The man was pointing a gun at them.

The old man moved toward the scene and soon recognized the girl and boy. "Abdul. Dalia."

He knew there was no time to waste. He threw himself toward them.

Dalia drew in one shaky breath, awaiting when the man would pull the trigger, after only a second had passed. *Don't make me wait in agony.* She looked over her shoulder at the cliff's edge, only a few feet from where she sat. *Should I throw myself over it?* But before she could decide, she felt a rush of air from behind her. Dalia tensed and looked in front of herself and her lifeless brother. There in front of them, was a man shielding them.

He briefly swiveled his head to glance at her, but it was enough time for Dalia to recognize him. *Is that my grandfather? Oh it is!* Dalia hugged him tightly. As she felt tears erupt from her eyes once again. Words could not describe the relief and pain that filled her as she held onto him.

The man, still holding the gun, looked as confused as ever, but then, his face turned into one of realization. He began to breathe heavily and rapidly. "You're still alive?" he said, as he looked at Dalia's grandfather with surprise.

THE VOICELESS DREAM

Dalia didn't need to look at her grandfather to know that horror was written all over his face. *He recognized him too! Will he die?* The man quickly brought his gun back up and pointed it at her grandfather. His hands trembled as he began to pull the trigger, his eyes wide.

"NO!" Dalia breathed, clutching him.

But nothing she said or did could help anything now. The trigger was pulled, and the shot rang in her ears loudly, cutting away nearly every last grip she had on her reality. Her grandfather tensed, froze, and then his hand grabbed at the ground, with his other hand on his chest.

Dalia watched in disbelief as he fell to the ground beside her brother, with blood all over his robes, his eyes still wide open. She put her hands over her mouth, and felt tears drip onto them as she cried. Every fragment of her life, every person she had ever loved, her only family, were all falling to the earth, lifeless, dead, and gone.

The devil of a man began to move toward her. Dalia quickly looked up at him and then instinctively jumped away. He began to raise his gun again and aimed it right at her. Dalia abruptly stopped backing from him as her hand began to lose sensation of the ground again. She was right at the cliff's edge. She shakily drew in a breath as her hopeless tears spilled down her face, streaking it damp.

As the devil neared her however, he suddenly lost hold of his gun and tripped over her brother and grandfather's perished figures. Dalia felt her heart leap in fright as he fell forward toward her. She leapt away from him and the cliff. He only had time to cry out in surprise once as he sent himself and the lifeless forms rolling toward the cliff's edge. And then, in the span of a second, they all fell over the edge of the cliff into the deep darkness below. His cry was suddenly cut off. And then there was silence. Stillness. The only things left on the cliff were his gun, in the midst of the eerie pool of blood, and Dalia left with her mauled soul.

She didn't even know what felt real anymore. Screams pierced all throughout her head over and over, like waves crashing in a storm. It didn't seem to end. She threw her hands to the ground and let her tears drip onto the dirt beneath her. Her heart ached and throbbed horribly, as if it was discovering pain for the first time.

Suddenly, the screams in her head stopped, almost all in an instant. Only one voice involuntarily hissed in her head. *What are you doing, Dalia? Get up. They are coming. Get up. Run! Run!* Dalia's eyes widened, and she felt herself stand as her legs straightened. Then she turned around and felt herself sprinting, back towards her village. Back home. Every movement she made felt involuntary, as she ran onward.

And Then There Were None

She was still running through the quiet streets of her village. The only sounds in the dead silence of the night were her shoes that were kicking up dust, and her shaky breath as she cried. The dark winding streets of her village had been one of the many things she had longed to see for days, but she had imagined she would meet them again with her brother and grandfather still alive. Not dead at the base of a cliff.

Dalia's heart still hurt. That seemed to be the only real pain she felt. Her brother's blood was still soaked all over her, a darker red than that of her shirt. She kept running, until she finally reached her home. Dalia pushed the door open and ran quickly into the bedroom, wiping away her tears, even though they still kept coming.

The Voiceless Dream

She collapsed onto her brother's bed, and clutched his blanket. She held it tightly for a moment, and then she lifted her head up slowly and stood unsteadily, gripping her brother's thin blanket, and walked over to her grandfather's basket. Breathing heavily as she knelt down, she wiped away her tears once more and dug into the basket. Once she felt his key, she pulled it out. She stared at it laying in her palm, as she felt more tears push past her eyes and trickle down her face.

Her chest felt tight and coiled. The key her grandfather had treasured all his life. The key to his home, that he never got back. And now he was dead. He was gone. Dalia held the key to her chest with one hand, and gripped her brother's blanket tightly with the other. She laid her head and body down on the cold floor, as it sent shivers up her bare arms, letting her pain spill from her eyes, as her soul screamed silently.

And soon, as she closed her watery eyes, sleep swept it's wings over her broken figure, taking her deep into a dream.

In her dream, as she slept soundly, she was in the life she had always wanted; the life she had always needed. She looked to either side of herself and saw a smiling man and woman. Even though she didn't could not make out their faces, she could just feel, and knew, that they were her parents.

The sun shone everywhere, spilling its light like a waterfall over the whole scene she saw in front of her. She

THE VOICELESS DREAM

glanced again at her parents, and now beside them, was her grandfather and brother. Dalia felt her smile widen as she looked at them. She turned her attention back in front of her and saw a man riding a bike, pulling a cart full of beautiful flowers of every color. She smelled roses in the air as he passed by. She looked to her left and saw small children jumping and playing with each other.

Above her, white doves sailed in the blue sky. Everywhere she looked, she felt happiness and joy radiated towards her. She heard laughter and felt at peace as she walked with her family, down the cobblestone street.

The buildings along the street looked like that of her village, but much larger, with arched windows. Every now and then she would see an olive tree in an isolated spot away from the homes.

Her dream suddenly led her to their small home in the village. She and her family entered it. Dalia's mother turned to her, while the rest of her family stood around them.

"Dalia," she said softly.

"Yes?" Dalia answered.

Her mother suddenly embraced her. Dalia hugged her back, feeling confused.

"What if I told you that we will be leaving you for a little while . . . "

Dalia broke away from her mother's warm arms. "What do you mean? Where are you going?"

Her mother gave her a sad smile. "We have to leave you."

THE VOICELESS DREAM

At that moment, the entire room went pitch-black. The sun was gone, the sky was gone, and Dalia seemed to be the only breathing being left.

"Are you still there?" Dalia whispered. She wanted her mother to hold her again. She wanted to rid herself of the foreboding feeling winding around her heart.

And then screams filled the room. The types of screams you hear when someone is being murdered. The types of screams that haunt you, tear you, and make you want to cease your own existence. Dalia had never felt more petrified in her life. She heard rushing around her, loud boots pounding on the floor and those horrid gun shots. And then everything was cut off with an abrupt silence.

Someone stabbed her in her chest. The striking pain stole the last thing she had. Her life. She fell back as the knife was drawn sharply out of her body and heard the footsteps of the murderer leave her. She was all alone. Again.

"Dalia!" someone yelled. The voice was filled with terror.

"Dalia! Dalia! Wake up!"

Dalia immediately sat up, sleep still swimming in her head, and put a hand at her temple. For some reason, the stab wound from her dream still hurt. The strange pain lingered. Her eyes focused and revealed a woman in front of her. It was the medic of her village, Rahan. "What is it?" Dalia asked fearfully, now growing extremely alert.

"We have to leave now! They are bombing us! Fire is everywhere! We will die!"

THE VOICELESS DREAM

Dalia frantically stood up, still holding her grandfather's key, and gripped Rahaf's hand as they ran out of her home. As they stepped out of the house, Dalia saw only orange haze and fire surrounding many homes. Everyone in the village was screaming and running, with parents holding their crying children, and other kids running away with their school books.

"What happened?" Dalia yelled as they ran, their path blurred by smoke.

"We're being bombed. Other villages around us are too."

Dalia felt perplexed. She felt immensely frustrated. "But weren't they supposed to patrol tonight?"

"Apparently not! Why would they get near the village when bombs and missiles will fall over it?"

As Rahaf uttered those words, Dalia realized what had happened, and why the soldiers had left the facility and their bases earlier. They kept running, trying to find an open path out of the village, but the smoke and heat delayed them. All Dalia heard were hurt cries piercing the night sky every second, and people yelling out of fear and grief. She and Rahaf had nearly tripped over several unmoving bodies lying on the pathway both of small children and adults, and many other people lying on the road weeping and wounded. Rahaf glanced to her right and then pulled Dalia forward, and abruptly to the left.

"Look out!" she shrieked. A house, only meters from where they had been running had exploded. Dalia stood up from where she had fallen, and she and the medic immediately increased their run to a sprint through the haze and confusion.

Everything was happening all at once, and she could not grasp it at all. Her home was most likely completely destroyed by now, just as all of the homes around her were. She was surrounded by rubbles of stone which had been homes, with more smoke rising from them. Her eyes stung horribly from the heat and the gas in the air, as if a knife had cut them.

Rahaf turned to her and spoke in a rush. "Dalia, I need to help everyone that's injured here and try to evacuate as many people as I can. You'll have to make it out of the village yourself. Just follow the road to the end and then take the last turn! Go now! Go!" Dalia watched as the medic bolted back the way they came. She pivoted around and forced herself to move forward.

Chaos was everywhere. Innocent dead souls were everywhere. Fire kept spreading and destroying the homes and lives of those all around her, including her own. Nothing made any sense. She felt so lost and broken, as if she had been torn into strips of nothing but burdening memories. Dalia wished with all of her heart to be back in her dream, but now that would never happen. Her dream was gone now, and it seemed almost as nonexistent as her happiness. The last shreds of her faith and perseverance were frantically clinging for existence onto her dream. Her beautiful dream. Her voiceless dream.

To Be Continued . . .

Keep reading for a preview of the next book:

RESILIENCE

The city. It was large and cramped. There were parts of the city that he liked. The vendors with their delicious food and drinks, the beautifully shaped homes and buildings at the heart of it, the restaurants, and the winding roads and paths that led to serene alleys. He liked the palm trees that were scattered around the city, and he enjoyed their shade even more. If the day was beautiful enough, the wind would pick up and bring a cool breeze to dance around the people bustling on the roads. The sun seemed to never want to sleep.

But there were other parts of the city that were darker places. On the eastern side, the city wasn't as bright as it should have been. Buildings with their concrete chipped off and electricity wires that hung like vines in the ominous alleyways lived in that part of the city. There were dreary corners where a threat could be awaiting. Sometimes the eastern side was welcoming, but too many conflicts had begun erasing its beauty a long time ago. The vendors weren't as common there, but their food was still delicious. Their meals and snacks were the only things that made the eastern side a bit more bearable.

But right now, he was not near the quiet alleys, the vendors, or the eastern side. He was outside of the city, with only the tricky terrain, sparse vegetation, and clouded sky as his companions. He had awaited this day for months, but he dreaded it as well. He gazed down at the dirt beneath him and inhaled, trying to smother his feelings. It didn't work.

"Ugh," he murmured. Suddenly, a breeze whisked past him for a few seconds. It sent chills up his arms, but he didn't mind. The sun had been baking the city for days. He gazed back up at the path ahead of him. The cemetery was in the distance.

After a short while, he neared the cemetery's gate. It was open. *Strange*, he thought. But he didn't allow his thoughts to inquire any more about the gate. He walked past it and entered the rows of graves. The stones were all rectangular. He ignored their inscriptions and the flowers that were atop the mounds they marked. He made his way to the end of the graveyard, where the last grave was only feet from touching the fence.

He stopped in front of that last grave. It was very unkempt. Weeds had grown from the dry ground and were tangled above it. The flowers that had been left there months ago were wilted and only a few of their dry petals remained. The inscription on the grave was the only thing that didn't look worn.

He walked around to the other side of the grave and placed his hand on the worn and uneven stone. He kissed the top of the gravestone lightly.

At that instant, he felt a drop of water hit the back of his hand. He slowly lifted his gaze to the sky and thunder rumbled. *It hasn't rained in so long.*

The rain began coming down fast after a few minutes. The raindrops splattered onto his shirt. It was raining harder and harder each moment. The sky was getting darker. He looked down at the grave and saw that it was damp and that there was not one place of dry stone that the rain hadn't touched. It had washed away the dust that had been coating the gravestone. As he looked down at it, water began dripping from his hair. He realized he was nearly drenched. His shirt was stuck to his skin. He shivered and lifted his head slightly.

Rainwater trickled down his face, streaking it wet. The rain smelled so fresh. He inhaled its scent and felt tears prick the back of his eyes. They escaped his brown eyes and followed the raindrops down his tanned skin, falling onto the ground beneath him where the rain was bouncing on the earth.

He kept his stare on the inscription in front of him as the results of his silent agony mixed with the water on his wet face and dripped off of it. That was one thing he admired about the rain. It washed away his tears. It washed away all the dirtied surfaces it touched and led them away. But it never stripped away his misery. Nothing did. Nothing would.

Author's Note

I wrote this book to portray the suffering that a large number of Palestinians experience. The Palestine-Israel conflict is a conflict that exists in the world today and is said to be a very complicated topic, but I believe it isn't as complicated as it is made out to be. I've read history books on the conflict, visited many human right websites, and have witnessed videos from a number of other sources and it almost always seems that the suffering from conflict is most heavily felt on the Palestinian side (as some accurate statistics have also shown).

The Palestinians face severe discrimination, police and military brutality, and continue to get their identities erased. Their real oppressors seem to be the Zionists, more specifically those that support the Israeli government. It also appears that a large portion of the Israeli military (the Israel Defense Forces) constantly kills innocent Palestinians at alarming rates, as studies, statistics, and other sources have shown. Their constant shootings seem too casual or purposeful to necessarily be deemed "accidental."

I know that not all Israelis are opposed to the Palestinians, and for sure the Jews are not to blame for their suffering. As a Muslim, I am proud to say that the Jews are our Quaran'ic cousins. However, there is just such a large number of Israelis that are opposed to the Palestinians and this opposition continues to propel discrimination against them.

If you do not know much about this conflict, have never heard of it, or just need more information on its history, then I encourage you to view my website on the conflict. My information website (meaning the website on this conflict) is contained in my author website and covers the history of the conflict, of which was obtained through history books, and also provides a page that proves that the suffering of the Palestinians is real through its credible sources, which contain human rights sources.

Also, I will emphasize again that this book is, in part, a work of fiction. However, every event in this story that occurred to the Palestinians that is *non-fictional* includes: the arrest (as well as treatment towards Abdul during the arrest) and treatment durring interrogation of Abdul (as well as the electric shocks he received), the events of the protest and the events surrounding it, the bombing, parts of the patrolling (routines), the dogs, and the tearing down of Palestinian homes. (Also know that the homes of Palstinians are torn down due to them not having the correct permit for their buildings, however, according to my reasearech, and statistics, Israel makes these permits nearly impossible for any Palestinian to obtain, and they do not provide an alternative shelter for the Palestinians afterward. More information on this can be found on my website.)

Made in the USA
Columbia, SC
11 September 2022